ALSO BY ELIZABETH COX

Night Talk
The Ragged Way People Fall Out of Love
Familiar Ground

BARGAINS IN THE REAL WORLD

RANDOM HOUSE • NEW YORK

Elizabeth Cox

BARGAINS IN THE REAL WORLD

Thirteen Stories

The following stories have been previously published: "The
Third of July" appeared in *Story* magazine; "Bargains in the
Real World" appeared in *The Rough Road Home: Stories by North
Carolina Writers* (Chapel Hill: University of North Carolina
Press, 1992); "Old Court" was originally read on National
Public Radio in 1989 and subsequently published in *American
Short Fiction* (Austin: University of Texas Press, 1990); "The
Singers" appeared in *The Crescent Review*; "A Sounding Brass"
appeared in *Antaeus*; "Land of Goshen" appeared in *fiction
international*; "Snail Darter" appeared in *Familiar Ground*;
"The Last Fourth Grade" appeared in different form in
The Boston Globe.

The excerpt by Mary Oliver on page ix is from *American
Primitive*, published by Little, Brown & Company.

Grateful acknowledgment is made to Graywolf Press
for permission to reprint an excerpt from *Night Talk* by
Elizabeth Cox. Copyright © 1997 by Elizabeth Cox.
Reprinted by permission of Graywolf Press.

Library of Congress Cataloging-in-Publication Data is
available.

ISBN 0-679-46329-1

Printed in the United States of America on acid-free paper
Random House website address: www.atrandom.com
9 8 7 6 5 4 3 2
First Edition

Book design by Victoria Wong

For all my students

Listen, whatever it is you try
to do with your life, nothing will ever dazzle you
like the dreams of your body,

its spirit
longing to fly . . .

"Humpbacks," MARY OLIVER

Acknowledgments

I want to express deep gratitude to my agent, Susan Lescher, who has encouraged me, supported me book after book, and given me good advice. I thank my editor, Pamela Cannon, who has read this book so many times and has made suggestions for which I am grateful. I acknowledge the help of my friend Kittsu Greenwood; my daughter, Beth Cox (who turns out to be a fine editor herself); and my son, Michael Cox. I'm grateful to Duke University for the opportunity to teach while I write. And special thanks to my husband, Michael Curtis, for his enduring love and support.

Contents

BARGAINS IN THE REAL WORLD

The Third of July

The night kept up one of those almost-silent rains until dawn, and now the mist rose and leaves showed their waxy shine. Nadine combed her hair but decided not to wash it. She pulled on her skirt and the blouse with cornflowers, and put away the pile of sewing she had promised to finish before tomorrow. Nadine was a seamstress. People brought their clothes to her to hem and make alterations.

Today was the third of July. Harold had left early for the field and would work late so he could take off all day on the Fourth. Nadine prepared a lunch for herself and another one for Miss Penny. Two days a week she took lunch to Miss Penny, and she would take it today. The old woman was like a mother to Nadine, ever since the year her own mother died, when she was nineteen. The year Bill was born too early. She put chicken salad and sliced tomatoes in a small basket made by Bill when he was six years old. She placed two pears inside and thought of the day he had handed it to her.

Nadine Colby had been married for thirty years, but on this morning she wrote a note to Harold after he left. *Dear Harold, I have rented an apartment in Mebane and if you want to see me you can call and ask to come by. Things cannot go on as they have.* She signed it *Love.*

A shaft of sunlight moved into the bedroom as Nadine packed her bags and put them into the car. She had already paid a month's rent for an apartment ten miles away in Mebane. Her sister lived nearby, but Nadine did not like her brother-in-law, so the apartment was a perfect alternative.

She left the note in a conspicuous place on the counter. Harold would see it when he came in. She fixed some dinner that could be heated up—a plate of meat loaf, potatoes, and creamed corn. Nadine wondered now if he would still take the whole next day off.

Her reason for leaving was based on one small happening: Harold came in one night, and though she knew who it was when he got out of the truck and started toward the house, Nadine thought he was someone different. His hair stuck up on one side, and he carried his cap, which he usually wore into the house and threw down on the hall table. But on this particular evening she thought he was a stranger, someone coming with bad news— telling her Harold was dead, or hurt. She imagined herself falling into the arms of this stranger and letting him hold her. All of these thoughts came in a few moments while Harold opened the door and said, "Whoa! It's hot!" Then she recognized his voice.

That night Nadine couldn't sleep. She lay next to Harold beneath the sheet and wondered how her life would be without him. If she left, it would have to be quickly and quietly, as though there had been a murder she could do nothing about.

He was foreign to her now, as was Bill. Her son was thirty and had been the reason they got married. Harold and Nadine had planned to have four children, though Bill was the only one.

The last time he came home Nadine said, "You don't look a thing like your daddy anymore, you know that?" She picked him up at the airport on Easter weekend. "Not a thing like him. And you used to favor him so strong."

"Lotta changes" was all Bill said.

"No one but me would know you was even kin."

Bill rode next to his mother with his long legs cramped in front of him. He had offered to drive, but Nadine insisted on doing so herself. She wore a navy-blue dress with a large white pin at her bosom, bought especially for Bill's visit. She felt pretty as she drove him home.

Bill was a salesman for MetroLife Insurance Company, and he had purchased this car for his parents—a Chrysler New Yorker. He had driven it into the driveway one Saturday and said it was theirs. Everyone in town knew Bill was wealthy and that he had bought them a car.

Their son came home on the Fourth. He also made regular visits for Christmas and Easter, but this year he would not come in July. Nadine told him he was getting stingy, though she meant self-centered. She had loved telling people how Bill always spent certain days with them and how she could count on him. But now Bill lived with a woman executive in his insurance company, and they were going off somewhere for the Fourth.

"I don't know what's going to happen if that woman gets pregnant," Nadine told Harold.

"They'll probably get married, like we did." Harold didn't think things had changed all that much, but he remembered when Nadine had seemed soft. Her softness had unraveled with the years, and he felt left with just a thin wire of who she was. But he never mentioned it. He loved his wife, even her sharp tongue. And he loved the way she sometimes exploded with laughter at something funny he said.

Yesterday, at breakfast, Harold read the paper and Nadine stared at the page that blocked his face. She imagined how he might speak to her, if he knew she was going to leave. *Nadine,* he spoke in her mind, *don't leave. Please don't.* He would beg. He would kiss her, then kiss her again, hard.

Yesterday, when he put down the paper, he asked, "What're we gonna do on the Fourth?"

Nadine didn't know at the moment how much she wanted out. She did not want to spend the Fourth of July with him. She would write a note on the third and let him go. As she thought of it, she felt like the ghost of someone, more than a real person.

"Anything," she said.

Harold kissed her cheek and left for the field.

Nadine washed the dishes and poured the rest of her coffee into the azalea bushes. She wanted to pick up the dry cleaning in town before going to Miss Penny's house.

She had not gone five miles before coming upon an accident.

A Ford station wagon had speeded past her only a few minutes before, and Nadine marveled at how this grief might have been her own. When she arrived at the wreck there was still a vibrancy lingering, as after a bell.

The car collided with a truck carrying chickens. It was the kind of crash that occurs in movies, where an audience roars with laughter as some fat farmer gets out stomping the ground and flapping his arms and elbows about—moving as the chickens themselves might move.

She hoped to see that now, even looked for someone to climb out of that screaming chicken truck, but as she drew closer she saw the driver tucked over the wheel. The station wagon's front end looked crumpled and the man driving had been thrown clear. He lay sprawled in the road. Nadine heard him groan for help and felt glad the car had not been her own.

She looked both ways for help, but no one was coming in either direction. She could not hurry toward the accident, her arms and legs felt like rubber bands. The man in the road was barely conscious. She stood over him, then squatted and placed her fingers on the pulse of his neck. She had seen this done on TV.

"My family," the man said. It was a question. He pointed toward the car as though he thought maybe Nadine hadn't noticed it yet. His head lay turned at a peculiar angle.

"Quiet now. You lie quiet." She patted the man's shoulder as if he had a contagious disease, then she moved back. He pointed again to the car. There was no sign of blood and Nadine hoped he was all right. "I'll check them for you," she said. The man seemed grateful to her and closed his eyes.

The man in the truck was slumped at the wheel. Four crates of chickens had fallen onto the hood. One of the chickens flapped around, but less now. There were more crates in the ditch where others squawked and fought to get free.

She heard another sound, which came from the car. Gurgling. A woman weighing almost three hundred pounds lay across the backseat. She had been sleeping when the accident occurred. Her head was on a pillow and she lay covered with a lightweight blanket, which was soaked with blood. Nadine, who always turned away from such sights on TV or in a movie, opened the car door.

The woman was drowning; the gurgling noise came from her own throat, which lay exposed by a low-neck dress, her skin white, supple. Nadine ducked into the backseat to help, and she thought how this woman must be about her own age. The effort for breath came closer now. But the woman's hands jerked as a child's does in deep sleep, and the top of her head was pushed askew, so that it hung precariously like a lady's small hat about to fall off.

Without even thinking, Nadine reached two fingers into the woman's throat and began to dig out debris. She dug again and again as though she were clearing out the hole of a sink. The woman began to cough and as she did her eyes opened—unseeing.

Nadine could see the place where the forehead split. She reached to put it straight, and the man from the road called out again about his family. Nadine said, "They're fine. You be quiet now." It was the calmest voice she had ever heard. She continued to clean the woman's throat, making her cough a few more times before the breathing came back. "You'll be all right," she told the woman, in case she could hear.

A young boy in the front seat curled slightly forward. About sixteen, Nadine thought. She got out to open the other car door, wiping her hands on her skirt. Some of the chickens wrestled free of their crates and walked around in the road. Another one had flown to a low branch. She glanced to the man at the wheel of the truck. He still hadn't moved. She wished he would.

She searched the highway, but there was no sign of help. As she opened the front car door, she expected to find the boy as she had found the woman, but only a small amount of blood trickled onto his shirt and pants. The dashboard had struck his chest, and he leaned forward onto it like a mannequin. He wore shorts and his strong legs had planted themselves to the floor as he braced for the impact. His arms caught the dashboard, but had fallen to his side as the dashboard caught him. The windshield had shattered and coated him with a shower of glass that spread as fine as Christmas glitter. Nadine wondered if he had ever played football.

When she looked up, she could see Emmett Walker coming across the field. She felt happy to see him, though she did not usually wish to see Emmett. In fact, she went out of her way to avoid him. Emmett wore coveralls and his red hair was almost completely gray. His arms and face, though, still showed his freckles from boyhood. Once, for three weeks, Nadine and Emmett had been sweethearts. Nadine could not imagine that now.

"I heard the crash from the field," he said. "Are they all dead?" He stared at the boy's shimmering back.

"Seems so" was what Nadine said, forgetting about the man in the road. She held her mouth as though it were full of food, then pointed to the woman in the backseat. Emmett peered through the window without commenting.

He turned to the chicken truck. "What about him?"

"I don't know." They walked toward the truck. Nadine wondered if she would be left here all day with Emmett and what she would do. They had seen each other in town, and at gatherings spoke pleasantly. Now they were suddenly talking in concerned tones and moving together as parents through a room full of sick children.

Emmett pried open the door of the truck. The man's face was hidden by the horn, but his eyes were open and his lips moved in an effort to speak.

"Listen," said Emmett, and he put his head closer to the steering wheel. "He's not moving. Something's wrong with his neck."

They went to each of the bodies, Nadine speaking low, explaining. But as she started to open the door of the car where the woman lay, they heard a siren approaching. Emmett put his hand on Nadine's shoulder and pointed to the ambulance coming over a far hill, arriving more slowly than the siren made it seem.

"I called the hospital," Emmett said.

Nadine went to stand beside the man in the road. He began to scream the name of his wife: *"Mamie, Mamie!"*

"Shhh," she told him. The ambulance driver and his attendant secured the stretcher beneath him, then called for Emmett's help. The man asked again about his family, and Nadine said not to worry. "Everything will be taken care of now."

"Somebody's still in the truck," Emmett said, and pointed to the tucked figure. "He's not moving." The attendant nodded and motioned toward the car, as if asking a question. Emmett shook his head and the driver reached into the backseat to check the woman's pulse. He stared boldly at the odd hairline.

"She's still alive," he said to Emmett.

Emmett peered through the window expecting—he didn't know what—maybe for the woman to sit up and say something.

"Wouldn't be, though." The driver directed his eyes toward Emmett. "Who did this? *You?*" The floor was full of Nadine's work.

Emmett looked at Nadine. She had her back to them as though the whole scene were something she had not yet witnessed.

"Hey, lady. You do this?"

She retreated the way a child does who has been reprimanded, her tongue in her cheek, worried. She nodded and held their admiration, then walked toward them, fragile and blue as smoke.

"Well, you saved her life, lady." He spoke softly and to the side, so that only Nadine could hear him, then he amended his statement. "Might have saved her life."

It took all three of them to lift the woman from the car, then Nadine stood back as they tore the front seat apart, trying to pull the boy from the dashboard. She wished she knew his name and hoped she had saved Mamie's life. They placed the son and the father in the back of the ambulance and Mamie next to them. The man from the chicken truck was strapped near the front. Everyone looked dead.

As the ambulance disappeared, Nadine and Emmett stood

beside each other. What followed was a silence as pure as that between lovers. Then Emmett faced Nadine and she turned to Emmett, and they resembled people who see their reflections in a mirror, slouched in a way they never imagined themselves.

Nadine opened her mouth and said, "I hope that woman lives. You think she will?" She wondered if she should take Emmett's hand or touch him, but didn't.

"Yes." He went to the truck, where chickens were scattered in the road. They had stopped their squawking. One was still in the tree. "I'll drive these over to Hardison's Poultry." He pulled the crates together. "What's left of them." He picked up the crates from the road and climbed into the truck. He turned the key several times before hearing it catch. As he drove off, he waved good-bye and Nadine waved back. She walked to the car and checked the salad. It was still cool.

Miss Penny was watching TV when Nadine arrived. She didn't hear the knock on the door, so Nadine walked in and called to her. Miss Penny was folding towels and placing each one beside the chair, fixing them like small bales of hay about to be stored in a barn. She was watching a game show.

When she lifted her head to respond to Nadine's voice, the pupils of her eyes were large and gave an expression of spectral intensity—hollow, not sad. A cataract operation had made them sensitive to light, so the blinds and drapes were pulled. The room, after the full sunlight of the road, seemed to Nadine unusually dark.

"I'll put this in the kitchen." Nadine patted Miss Penny's

chair as she walked by. She wanted to scrub her hands and wipe her skirt clean.

"There's a man on here who'll win ten thousand dollars if he can answer this last question," Miss Penny said. Nadine took it as a silencing. The TV blared the question and the announcer declared him winner. Bells rang, people clapped and cried, and Miss Penny told her, "I could've won me ten thousand dollars." She pushed herself from the chair to go to the kitchen.

"Don't know what you'd do with it," said Nadine. She watched the old woman hobble to the kitchen and fall into a chair.

"I'd buy me something."

"Don't know what you need to buy." Nadine spooned salad onto plates and set two places at the table. Her tongue felt dry and she asked Miss Penny if there was some iced tea. Miss Penny pointed to a pitcher. She always made tea and took out the ice trays before Nadine arrived, but today Nadine was two hours late and the ice was mostly water. She put the slivers that remained into the tea and sipped it.

"I had the right answer," Miss Penny persisted. She tasted the salad, and Nadine gave her a napkin.

"You can't spend the money you have now, let alone ten thousand dollars." They helped themselves to the tomatoes. "What would you spend it on?"

"I'd pay somebody to look after my dogs."

"You don't have any dogs," said Nadine, "and don't need any."

"I would if I had all that money." Miss Penny's words, though simple, were true. "I'd need a lot of things." She thought for a moment, chewing her food with meticulous care. "I'd get some dogs. Not the regular kind, but show dogs. The ones you can train and take to shows."

"You'd like that?" Nadine asked, surprised to learn of a new interest held by a woman she had known as long as she could remember. She had thought there were no more surprises left between them.

"Show dogs." Miss Penny's face flushed at the thought of it. "I always have wanted to do something like that."

Nadine wished to say something about the accident, to tell someone what she had done and how she wasn't afraid to see Emmett anymore. "There was a wreck," she began, and leaned across the table so Miss Penny could hear. "Over near Hardison's Poultry. A truck ran into a station wagon. The whole family got hurt." Miss Penny reached for more slices of tomato. Her face had not yet lost its flush. "It was pretty bad," Nadine said. "A man and his wife, a boy about sixteen."

"What?"

"Their *son* about *sixteen*." Nadine spoke louder. "He was killed right off, but the man might live, and the woman—" She stopped leaning and slumped back. "I don't know about the woman, though." Nadine's gaze shifted to something outside the window.

"Ten thousand dollars," Miss Penny said. Her voice emphasized each word equally.

From the kitchen window Nadine could see bags of web in the crab apple trees. "Tomorrow's the Fourth of July," she told Miss Penny. Neither of them turned away from the window.

Nadine washed a few dishes and put away the towels into

the hall cabinet. She decided not to go to Mebane but to go back home. "I'll put these pears in the refrigerator." She held up the pears. Miss Penny's eyes unclouded and hardened clear as stones.

On her way home, she picked up the dry cleaning and stopped at the pet shop to look at dogs not yet full-grown. On Tuesday she would buy one and take it to Miss Penny. He would outlive her by six years.

The note to Harold had not been touched, but she left it propped against the sugar jar. The house looked older now. Each object seemed to have a separate life of its own. When Nadine saw herself in the mirror over the fireplace, she became aware of the frame around her face.

She called the hospital, but the line was busy. She had already unpacked her bag and put the clothes into drawers where they had been—her blouses, her good blue dress, two night-gowns, a sweater, four pairs of shoes. She put her umbrella in the hall closet and went to sit across from the large picture window.

Twilight made the room silver, drapes shimmering like creek water. The late sun dropped halfway from sight, going down behind the trees like some wild head, and Nadine wondered if everyone wished for life to be different.

When the phone rang, it was Emmett. She heard his voice, and her mouth worked itself into a smile. He called to tell her about Mamie and Robert Harkins. "The man will live," he said. "And the woman, she'll live too." For a moment Nadine could not even straighten her legs. "But that boy, he didn't make it. He was dead when we saw him."

"What about the man in the truck?"

"His back was broke, and some ribs. But he's all right, or will be." Emmett coughed as though he didn't have much to say but wanted to think of something. "The truck driver was Buck Hardison's nephew."

"Why, I think I know him," Nadine said. "I think I met him once when he was a little boy." She wanted the conversation to go on, and she thanked Emmett, so he said she was welcome. "You were fine to help," she told him through the silence in the cord. "I mean, really," and she spoke as if trying to convince him of something important.

"Well," said Emmett.

Nadine watched the sun go all the way down and wondered if Emmett had turned to see out his own window. "It's getting dark," she said.

When they hung up, Nadine sat until she could see nothing but her own reflection in the window, and the reflection of the lamp beside her. Harold would be in soon. She decided to wash her hair. She was bending her head over the sink and rinsing for the second time when she heard him.

"Nadine?"

She wrapped her hair in a towel and went to the kitchen. Harold held the note that Nadine had not thrown out. He held it but didn't say anything.

"You want something to eat?" she asked him.

Harold said he did.

Nadine did not get the covered plate of meat loaf and creamed corn. Instead, she took out some flounder and began to prepare it for baking with lemon and butter. She cut up new potatoes to go with it and told Harold about the wreck.

She told about the man, the boy, and the woman she saved, the truck driver who was Buck Hardison's nephew. She told him she had seen Emmett and how they had worked together. Her telling went from the time she took out the fish, cooked it, to when she sat down with Harold to eat.

The note lay on the counter as they talked. Harold had carefully placed it next to the sugar, facedown. He listened attentively and ate everything Nadine put before him. When she was through washing the dishes, he walked up behind her to turn her around. He slowly unwrapped the towel from her head. Her hair was damp and frizzy, and he rubbed it dry with his hands.

Old Court

The room, even at midday, held a romantic dimness as though it were always lit by a lantern. Sunlight hit the dark wood floor and mahogany table in a way that gave the room a yellow glow, and the optical illusion of a lantern was strong when the wind blew, changing the shadows so that light fought itself like boxers against the walls. But even with all the sunlight, there were corners that remained unlit.

Three chairs were arranged around a rug. The larger, more comfortable chair was my mother's; so was the table beside it—her favorite, made of cherrywood. She kept her sewing on that table and would never let a glass or a bottle be set upon it. As I remember her table, and the yellow light of that room, it stands in my mind like a dream, becoming immemorial and ancient as a court.

·   ·   ·

The Civil War had been over for three years when my father died. I was nine, too young to be the man of the house. Sometimes my uncle would come. He put his hand on my shoulder as if I were a grown man, and I liked for him to be there.

During our last summer and fall in that house, a shift of happenings began to occur. I was eleven then. Men came by on horseback. Strangers. They arrived in a flurry, as birds would, the horses jostling even as the men jumped from them. We never knew when to expect their arrival. This time, I could see from a low windowsill and count six of them, at least, all going to the back of the house to dip one by one from the well. They could have just as easily robbed us. My mother's jewelry box did not have much, but had a gold wedding band, and a watch with three diamond chips, and two pearl earrings given to her by an aunt who lived in New England.

There had been a light snow the night before, though it was October and unusual for cold weather to come that early in Mississippi. Marigolds still bloomed in the fields. The snow came around five in the morning but melted and was gone by ten.

"They've come back," I yelled toward the other room. My mother knew, her ears attuned to every danger. We lived in the house alone, miles from town. All we had was the house, our garden out back, my mother's job at the piece-goods store, and small jobs I could take in summer months, a field lying fallow, and these men rushing to our well in bad times. The well had not filled up yet after the summer's drought. We had barely enough water for ourselves, and them taking all they could, then heading out—my mother relieved each time.

"We must go away soon," she would say, but found it hard to leave.

And when the men came, she hid herself where she could see the door but where she wouldn't be seen. She held a shotgun loaded and ready, pointed at the door. I often wondered if she would have turned herself loose to kill or maim, if she would actually pull back the trigger.

"They've come back," I yelled again, but I could see her already crouched between the large chair and table. Her hair was pulled up into a braid on the crown of her head, and she looked prettier than she had looked in months.

The men called obscenities back and forth, their talk like a thorn stuck in my mind. I hoped my mother wouldn't notice, thinking she must go out and grab them by their ears, swat each one for his remarks. In fact, I couldn't picture her failing to do this, so I wanted to warn them, lest she hear.

I knelt by the window, my eyes barely over the sill. I thought that only my eyes were over the sill, forgetting about the top of my head. The men walked around the yard in the openness of their desires. They wore boots in summer and they wore boots now, only now they wore heavy coats and caps that fit tightly around their heads. The strong, flatland wind gave their clothes a heavy flutter, and the caps made their eyes seem wide, blank as owls.

Each man drank from a dipper beside the well, and I laughed because it was the dipper I let my dog drink from. I wondered where Buster was, since he usually barked and snapped at them. One man picked up a piece of leather. It was part of my father's belt that I had cut to make a collar for Buster. I hoped the man wouldn't take that last scrap, but as I saw him tuck it into the side pouch of his saddle I tried to forget about it. I didn't know how many times they might come back to the house, or what else they might do. We lived halfway between two towns, and even when my father was alive men would ride by and ask for water—but they always asked.

When one of the men saw me at the windowsill, he ran and hit the wood frame to scare me. My mother moved in the next room. I felt the sudden queasiness one feels just before throwing up, so I lay flat against the floorboards. Upon hearing them leave, I relaxed enough to count the cracks on the wall and thought about when Uncle Josh would come.

My uncle came out on Saturdays. He had never married, though I think he had women he lived with from time to time. He was tall, like my father, and had dark hair that never looked combed. My mother's hair was straight. At bedtime when she brushed it a hundred strokes, her voice grew musical. I think it was the only time she thought of herself as pretty. She threw her hair over her face and brushed it from the nape of her neck, then pushed it back. It was so long she could sit on it. And at those times, she talked and asked questions or listened to whatever I said, without being busy, her expression as calm as soap.

My dad was a large man. I thought I would never be that large, and in fact I'm not. We duck hunted all winter—my dad and me and Uncle Josh—and always on Christmas Eve. Christmas Eve morning, before the light, we would rise and eat the cold ham biscuits my mother left out. She said she was not getting up at any four o'clock in the morning just to fix breakfast. But she would prepare biscuits late at night and wrap them already piled with ham and butter, so that in the morning they were good, if not warm. And she always called from the bedroom anyway, at four-fifteen, "You boys need anything?" so that we could tell her the biscuits were fine, maybe the best she had ever made, because she had been up later than we had, fixing them. We thanked her in that way so she fell asleep satisfied.

Our duck pond was not really a pond, but a slough, a natural marshland forty yards wide and good for ducks. On almost any Saturday morning in the late fall, Uncle Josh came by with hip boots and gear, and we waded the fields the way we had done with my father, breaking the ice in places. Josh broke it as he stepped, without thinking. I broke it on purpose, going whichever way I saw unbroken patches so I could break them and hear them crack.

Sometimes Josh brought other men with him, but usually he took only me. He taught me the difference between a birch and a poplar, and would tell stories of my father, how they rode together in the war. He told how they named their horses after women they loved and that my dad named his horse Ruby after my mother, saying if he was going into something he might not come back from he would go into it with Ruby. Each time Josh told me this he said it with such fervor that I wondered if that time of his life was the best and did he long for it. Once I asked him, and he stared at me for a moment as though I had shown him a truth he hadn't expected.

"Maybe," he said. He pulled me to stand close to him. "But I don't wish for it." Our hip boots touched. It was awkward to stand that close, because of our boots, but I stood, not moving. I even put my arm around his waist, not out of love but to keep from falling. He said, "I only meant to give you an idea of it, and how we were afraid."

"You never said about that."

"I didn't?"

"No."

"It was when you saw them coming," he began, and I settled in to listen. "Saw them coming toward you with what you had, maybe more, and bent on doing to you what you would do to them." His eyes went back to remember. "It killed something in me, and in your father, too, I think. Though not as much." He looked as though he were telling something different now. "I mean," he said, "the things we had to do."

I didn't know what he meant. "Those men came back," I told him. "They kicked Buster and hurt his ribs." Josh didn't say anything, and I wondered if he knew where he was and if we would hunt anymore that day.

We did. We hunted three more hours. The sun came all the way up but couldn't warm us because our boots and jackets were wet. Our bodies were dry, though, and warm enough, if not as warm as they would be. We walked back with greenheads hanging from the back satchels of our vests, and talked about how the house would smell like mincemeat and how the heat would hold our faces the same as the cold did, only better.

The table was set, the floor swept and slightly damp from being mopped. My mother met us at the door to prevent us from dragging in our boots. We left boots, shirts, and pants on the steps, and she made us wash up. It always struck me as strange that we had to be clean for meals, but it didn't matter much if we were dressed. My mother wore a skirt and flowered blouse. We wore long underwear, though Josh put on pants. If company came, I put on pants too.

"Your father is dead," my mother told me one day when I got in from school. She sat in a chair where she always sat, so that when I walked in from school she was what I saw first. I saw her that day, too, but she had her arms outstretched before her, leaning toward me, and I went into them as deep as I could. Then she pushed back, and I saw in her face the very root of her disbelief.

"How?" I finally asked, but she had already begun to tell me.

"He lifted lumber onto the wagon. A heavy load, mostly likely." She sounded admonitory, if not critical. "And it fell back on him," she said. "He climbed onto the wagon, and logs rolled across him. When they lifted the load off his chest, he was already gone." She began to cry softly. I wanted to but couldn't. Instead, I watched tears squeeze out from those tight-closed eyelids, falling quick and soft between us. She kept her arms around me, not even attempting to cover her face as I would have done. It was as though she could not be embarrassed or ashamed, only sad. She grieved for my dad better than I did, for I refused to bear it for almost a year. And finally, when I could talk of him and show tears, my mother's tears were gone.

The men on horseback came during the summer months and on that one October day, but it was Christmas Eve when they came by at night. My mother and I attended the Christmas pageant in town and got home late, ten o'clock. The men probably had been there already and found the house empty, not wanting anything there but wanting something to do with us, a mischief.

My mother would stay up late and put out whatever I received for Christmas, pretending still that it was brought in secret, both of us pretending, because there could be only one or two gifts, and the surprise was all. So we held to this, partly because she wanted to and never mentioned doing differently, and partly because I wanted to prolong the belief. Besides, most of the time my mother thought of me as a child. It was only now and then that she stood back, even stepped back physically from me, and said, "You look like your father when you do that," and she looked a little longer, not seeing him exactly, but seeing me in a different way. I always liked those times, because she wouldn't hug me to her as though she needed something I couldn't give anymore, but instead would ask me to perform some task that she said had become too difficult for her.

We were not home fifteen minutes before we heard them, the hooves and galloping we had heard before but always in the daytime. I had put on my pajamas, soft, heavy material that kept me warmer sometimes than my clothes. My mother still had not undressed, but she had set the table for the next morning's breakfast. I hoped she might brush her hair.

When I entered the kitchen, she put out the lamp. For a moment, neither of us could see, and she reached through the dark for me, whispering, "Luther, Luther."

"I'm here." But her hands had already found me.

"Get the shotgun." She went in another direction as I fingered my way toward the mantel and above it to where the shotgun hung. It was always loaded.

She came toward me again, both of us now able to see each other's shadows. The moon was full and the room flooded with its light. The floor shone white as water, and I almost expected, when I stepped, to hear the crack of ice.

I handed the shotgun to her. She took it with one hand, her arm seeming longer in the moonlight, thinner than it really was. With her other hand, she pushed something toward me.

"Merry Christmas," she said.

I could not see it but knew it was a rifle, and wondered how she would pay for it. A Winchester 66. It was what I wanted but hadn't imagined getting. I stroked the wooden stock and the silky black barrel, and felt sorry about the present I had for her. It wasn't enough.

The men had stopped their horses. They didn't go around to the well, nor did they come with the flurry of their usual visits.

"Is it loaded?" I asked.

She said it was.

I readied myself in a position below the sill, and wondered if I would have to kill a man and if it would kill something in me. I didn't feel the hate I thought I would need to feel. The door was being tried—no knock, just breaking in—and I felt a rising nausea.

I squeezed the trigger, not at the door but out the window. The breaking of glass was all I heard. I squeezed again and again and the shots came out like tears from those tight-closed eyelids. My mother called my name and at last, after what seemed an interminable wait, the noise leveled out against the night's quiet. But before full silence fell again, I could see in that holy Christmas light a horse rising up, then dropping, his legs crumpling as paper would, paper legs to hold his heavy body and head. And I heard his sound, after the sound the gun made, a whinnying too high-pitched for anything but pain. A pure calling for help, and his knees bending to that call.

"Damn." One man ran to the horse. "Damn." He looked down at it, a dark heap like coal. My mother came to the window. The man at the door yelled to his friend, and they both climbed onto the other horse. We watched as they rode off.

"They are drunk," my mother said. Her first words. But she was quiet about what I had done. And finally, when she lit the lamp, minutes after the men had galloped off, her face was like chalk. And she tried to praise me, as though what I had done was well thought out and what I had planned to do.

But it wasn't. It was what I did. And she thought I had decided to shoot but not to shoot at the man. She thought my mind had made the decision not to kill him.

"You decided," she said, giving me credit. "You made that decision from some old court in your mind. I am proud."

"But, Mama—"

"I am proud." She would always see me better than I was.

The next morning when I went out I knew I had to dig a hole big enough to bury the horse where he lay. He could never be moved, not by me nor my mother, so I dug most of the day, and later in the evening my mother helped. It took two days to dig a hole big enough to shove him into. By then the flies had come and the sun had begun to bake his skin.

My mother and I wore kerchiefs on our faces to keep from breathing the odor. We were glad the air was cold and kept the flesh from rotting too quickly. I had uncinched the saddle and was able to pull it from under the horse, but I couldn't loosen the bit from his mouth. His teeth had locked shut around it. Then I remembered my father opening a horse's mouth once by squeezing the sides where the mouth began, and when I did that, the bit fell out. We threw the bridle and saddle into the hole with him, and the halter strap, but I kept the blanket that had covered his back and protected him from sores.

The day we pushed him into the hole, it was raining. My mother packed our trunk and filled the wagon with all she could. Josh and the man from the piece-goods store came to help us bring our furniture to the new house.

We did not move far, but into town where there were lawns and neighbors. A few weeks went by before I remembered that I had failed to give my mother her gift. We rode back to the house, which no one lived in now but had been sold with the land. The mound of dirt rose fresh, and we shuddered to think what was beneath it. The door of the house had blown open, and snow or rain had ruined the front entrance. The romantic dimness had gone.

I climbed to pull a loose brick from the fireplace and removed a small, rectangular box wrapped in paper with shiny red flowers. My mother loved the paper and praised it. I watched and took the praise.

The box held a necklace, its pendant the shape of a leaf. It was yellow gold and opened like a locket. When she opened it, there was a picture inside, the only one I could find, which was of herself when she was ten years old.

She sat down on an old crate and I stood close beside her. "Put it on me," she said. So I did. She pressed it flat against her chest. Then she turned her head toward the window and fingered the leaf, opening and closing it to hear the soft click. But when she turned her gaze back to me, her eyes were so full of admiration that I felt like a small god. She put her hand on my back, and the smile that came to her face was like a crescent, each corner turning upward as if it had been drawn there.

I smiled too but tried to pretend I had smiled at something else—outside maybe—a bush. Then I looked to see the pane still broken, the simply rounded mound of dirt, the dark heap beneath it that would stay beneath me, like something I would have to stand on. But all around us the rest of the land lay flat, and as far as I could see, it went out straight before us.

The Singers, 1949

I know but little the process of these things
Yet I know the severed head still sings.
"Castle Tzingal," FRED CHAPPELL

There is a craving for chocolate that, when satisfied, produces something similar to the euphoria of being in love. Elvenia gave me chocolate every time I saw her, carried it in her pocket; but each time she gave me only one piece. I never gave anything to her, but never thought about it. As the daughter of a boarding school teacher, I lived on a hundred-acre campus that sat on a hill overlooking the Tennessee River. I knew every inch of the grounds and as a child was allowed to wander as far as the gates. All my life my mother said, "Don't go past the gates."

"Hey, Elvenia," I called. Elvenia worked in the laundry. A low brick wall surrounded the enormous tree rising out of cement beside the steps. That tree stood taller than the laundry and I often wondered, as I approached, how roots could grow so deprived of light.

The laundry doors were always open, even in winter. As I came close a hot, steamy blast of air hit my face. Inside, colored men and women worked behind large silver-gray machines. The machines made the people look small.

"Hey, Jenny." A colored woman shouted from the back of the laundry room and waved her thin arm. When she threw up her hand, I thought of a small bird moving away from a limb. Her hand fluffed the air until I waved back.

"Your clothes not ready yet," Elvenia said. I went to stand next to her and the machine. "It'll be a while." Elvenia was ironing shirts. A hiss went into the air as she smiled.

"Didn't come for clothes," I said. "I'm looking for Tyree. Mama wants more firewood. Kindling."

"Button your coat up, honey," Elvenia fussed, turning to button it for me herself. "That cold air gonna get in your throat and first thing you know you gonna be laid up in bed." Elvenia wore a short-sleeved light cotton dress no matter what the weather, and never had a cold that I knew of. "And who you think's gonna nurse you well?"

"You are."

She smiled and lifted strands of my hair, letting them fall through her fingers, showing it to people. Tommie Lou, Elvenia's cousin, stood behind me. "Look at that baby's hair." Elvenia turned my shoulders for Tommie Lou to hug. Her big arms reached around me and her dress opened at the neck to reveal her big bosoms. When I was almost a year old, and refused to eat for five days, Tommie Lou chewed up sweet potatoes with sugar and fed me her chewed-up food eight times a day, until I was strong. My mother told me that that was all I would eat, and that she watched Tommie Lou feed me like a baby bird.

"That stuff we have won't burn without kindling," I told Elvenia, and she went to a back room to find Tyree.

Elvenia was a tiny-framed woman whose head looked smaller than it was. She always wore a cap that mashed her hair down flat. When she walked she looked disjointed and moved with a force that made me wonder if she endured some kind of physical pain she never told anyone about. She walked as if she were stuck on pegs.

"He's coming in a minute," she told me, and settled in again to her work. Her feet found their place on the floor where comfort would come. "You're not supposed to be in here, you know. Don't tell your mama I brought you in here, or I won't bring you in again." She handed me a piece of Hershey bar from her pocket.

"I won't," I said. "Are you mad?" I nibbled the chocolate.

"No madder than I oughta be." She laughed, so I laughed too.

Tyree emerged from behind a curtain nailed to the top of a door-facing. He was tall and thin, with hair turned gray in places, but his face had stayed the same for years. He took my hand and we walked out together. I waved to Elvenia, but she forgot to look up.

Sammy, Elvenia's husband, signaled to me from the other side of the room. He was in charge of the laundry. He waved with his head, since his hands fed the largest machine. His arms reached high and pulled down a lever that could press a pair of pants in one swipe. Sammy's face dripped with sweat. He was a short, fat man with a huge mouth. Sweat dripped from his forehead and his nose.

Tyree's hands were thin and weak, not fat and sure like Tommie Lou's, not strong as wire like Elvenia's. I tried to keep in step with him and to think of something to say, but his face kept a hard expression. Every year his expression grew harder.

One day, while Tyree was putting up new wallpaper in my room, I asked him how old he was and he told me. I said I was eight. That was a year ago. He said he had a little girl once, and I asked where she was now. "She's dead," he said. "Well," I said, "sometimes I wish I would die." But it wasn't true. He said sometimes he wished it too. Then, while his arms were in the air, pressing the wallpaper, I reached around his waist to hold him. I don't know why I did it. My ear pressed against his shirt and when he brought his arm to rest on my shoulder, he pushed me gently aside.

As we headed toward the woodpile, Tyree asked, "How old are you now?"

"Nine."

"Whoo." Tyree said "whoo" no matter what question he asked or what answer I gave. I wondered what I could say that would move him, make him drop the wall that rose up the minute I was there and let down when I left. But I knew, looking at him, that nothing I could do, probably ever, could break down that guard. And I wondered what had stirred him, what had ever struck him hard and left its blow. He had asked me a question I didn't hear.

"What?"

"How's Miss Jane Ann?" Jane was my sister, who had left for college last fall. He called her Jane Ann, even though her name was just Jane.

"Fine."

"Whoo."

"She'll be home in March. It's her spring break."

"Mmm-hmm." Tyree shook his head as though I had told him something appalling.

Behind the library we picked up several bundles of kindling. He let me carry one, then asked me to stack bundles onto his arms. When we got to my house, he placed the packages of kindling on the front porch, putting them down carefully. He knew my mother would come out to give him money. She opened the front door to thank him and tucked dollar bills into the palm of his hand. He acted as though he didn't notice. Then she offered him a gift of cantaloupe she had been saving for herself. He accepted, but I thought he probably didn't like cantaloupe, and I felt sorry for my mother.

The next day was a holiday, one of those bright February days that made me think of peppermint. On holidays the campus was quiet, and I took long walks around the lake, wandering as far as the stables, as far as the gates.

As I walked, I counted each step I took to the lake, and then to the stables. I recorded the number in a small notebook. If a discrepancy occurred, I blamed the mistake on the shortness of one of my legs—deciding that maybe (on certain days) one leg proved to be shorter than the other, so my count would be thrown off. I imagined that my uneven gait was visible, though no one had ever mentioned seeing my limp. Some days I exaggerated the way I walked, so that the limp would be impossible not to notice. Still, no one mentioned it. I wondered if people were embarrassed to think that I had been a cripple all those years and they hadn't noticed.

At the laundry I saw the chain that wound around the huge knobs of the doors to keep them locked. Today, the chain hung loose, the door slightly ajar. I went to unwind the chain completely, to look in. The machines waited inside like large sleeping animals.

No one was there, but the room was filled with the clean smell of starch and steam, and I saw the curtain from behind which yesterday Tyree had emerged. I decided to peek into the room, and had visions of black kettles—huge, with water boiling inside. I pulled back the curtain, feeling that I was entering a dark belly, but the darkness was not in this room. It was behind my own eyes. I went in, and as I did, I felt the room was seeing me, and that I had walked in blind. I wished for a rush of heat to hit my face, but instead my head filled with the smell of cigarettes and stale food.

A bare bulb hung from a string in the middle of the room, and I stood on a chair to click it on. The click made my head feel clear, gave a neatness to my thoughts and an order to the room. I clicked it several times before climbing down.

A cot was pushed against the wall, the sheets rumpled and unmade. A desk was in the corner, and a lamp. The desk did not have drawers but opened from the top, and the name SONJA was scratched in block letters next to the inkwell. I lifted the top and found a package of Red Man Snuff and some magazines. Beside the radiator was a box with a garter belt, some stockings, a pair of worn slippers, and two empty RC Cola bottles. I touched the radiator. It was cold, but I could hear the pipes knocking like hammers, so I knew heat would come. Scattered all around the room were bowls scraped empty of food.

A tall chifforobe stood on the other side of the room. It had a narrow full-length mirror. I had never seen a piece of furniture that big. Opening the chifforobe doors, I found men's shirts, pressed and starched and buttoned all the way down. Beside the shirts hung a long yellow nightgown.

At the foot of the cot a large wicker basket spilled over with bright scarves and old clothes. I picked a green and yellow scarf to tie on my head and looped the ends of a big-flowered bedspread around my neck—a cape that draped to the floor. I pretended I was at a festival, and strutted back and forth in front of the mirror. I searched through the basket for a bracelet or rings and found an old cape of Elvenia's, but didn't try it on.

A noise made me turn, but even before turning I knew a man stood at the doorway. He was a young man, and he held back the curtain, leaning against the jamb in a way that made me think he had been there awhile. He was not someone I knew. In fact, I had never seen him before. I tried to say something that might ease the severity of his face and hoped he might speak first. But he didn't say a word. So I spoke, not to him, but to the straight-backed chair propped in the corner, its front legs sticking up off the floor.

"I was looking for something," I lied, though it didn't feel like a lie. And I thought he laughed, but it was more of a short breath pushing through his nose. He stepped into the room, in one large stride, and bumped his head on the hanging bulb, changing the way light fell into the room, making the room itself seem to sway. He took hold of the upper part of my arm. My arm was bare and thin where his fingers reached all the way around. I felt he could break it off like a wheat stalk if he wanted to.

He jerked at the green and yellow scarf hard enough to make my head snap back. The end of the scarf brushed my cheek and I put my hand there as though he had slapped me. He looked at the loop around my neck where the bedspread was tied. With my other hand I untied the loop so he would not jerk at it. The bedspread dropped to the floor with a soft sound that made the man stand still.

I do not know how long I stood like that before his hand reached between my thighs and groped. My arms hung at my sides, trusting the touch of men and women who offered their dull nurturing, but not understanding what he would do. He lifted me straight into the air and though his eyes didn't see me, he looked at my face as though he had decided to pay an old debt, then changed his mind, deciding to pay on half.

My body went up, stiff as a board, higher. "Shhh," he kept saying, as if he were hearing a great noise. I waited suspended in the air near the string wire, near his head. I could see his hair closely cropped, and his hairline as sharp as the boundary of a farmer's field. I wondered if this was his room. The heat hammered its way through the pipes and entered the room in short, heavy blasts. The man turned to the radiator's noise, his hands still kneading my groin. He looked neither angry nor pleased.

We could hear someone come into the laundry, walk toward the room, and the man put me down to shake a warning finger once in my face. Elvenia pulled back the curtain.

"Hi, Elvenia," I said. "Elvenia," I said again, to feel relief.

"Hi, honey." Elvenia stepped quickly and put her hands on my shoulders to make me face her. The man walked backward and raised his elbows against us. Elvenia looked only at me.

"What you doin' here," she said to me. It wasn't a question. "No place for you." She pushed my hair from my eyes with her thumb and the heel of her hand. "This is no place," she said. I could see our reflections in the chifforobe's long mirror. We seemed wavy and unreal.

"I wanted to see what was back here." My arms felt wet and heavy at my sides.

"And now you know." Her voice turned to an apology. "It ain't you, honey," she said, and hugged my shoulders.

"It *is* her." The man's voice came out coarse.

"Shush yourself." Elvenia's head turned toward the man with the quickness of a snake. "She's just a child." Then she said, "You're just like Sister. You are Sister's own boy in your madness." I didn't even know Elvenia had a sister.

"It *is* her, Elvenia."

Elvenia gave him a look and he shushed. Then she turned toward me hard for a moment, so I waited.

"You run along home now," she said to me in a voice that was soft but not kind. Still, I waited. Elvenia slipped off her shoes and rolled down her stockings. "I'm gonna take a nap," she told us both, dismissing us. She stopped the roll at her ankles and turned to me again as if she had just realized something important, but something that was impossible to apply to her life. "Tell your mama I've made some biscuits for tonight. I'll bring them over later." When she reached for the Red Man Snuff, I thought she was reaching for chocolate, but she didn't give me any chocolate before I left.

The man held back the curtain for me to walk out, but Elvenia said, "Stay here for a minute, Lyman. Don't leave with that girl." It took me a moment to realize that "that girl" was me.

I turned to see Lyman once more, to see his arm drop from the curtain before it closed. I never forgot it, his arm coming down as I came down to the floor, his hand beneath me, coming down from the bulb, from his furry head and his slow, driven stare. I walked halfway across the big laundry room, thinking that I should say something to them before I left, something to ease myself. Then I remembered.

"Elvenia?"

No one said a word.

Then, "Mmm-hmm?"

"They're going to give you and Tyree a gold watch at the next Awards Dinner." I had learned this secret two months ago and was pleased to tell Elvenia now. I thought the news might make up for breaking in to her back room, even though I hadn't taken anything.

A chair moved and a chifforobe door closed before Elvenia stuck her head outside the curtain. She still wore her cap.

"They gonna do what?"

"Give you a gold watch. Tyree too." I felt proud to say it. "My daddy says you *deserve* it."

"Lord." That was all she said before closing the curtain.

"Gonna give us a *go-old* watch," Elvenia sang. I hardly recognized her voice. It sounded more like a squawk.

Lyman laughed.

"You'll know the *ti-ime*," he sang back. "And you *de-serve* to know. To wear the *gol-den* watch. And say, '*This* is the *ti-ime.*'"

"A *gol-den* time. Whoo. We gonna *wear* that watch."

They sounded as if they were singing a song together. Closing the large doors to the laundry, I could still hear them singing.

Outside, I stood by the tree and tried to decide if I was different or the same. Even when the doors were completely shut and the chains were wrapped around the knobs, I could hear them through the small window. I have heard them for all my life.

Land of Goshen

As a mother, Sara was incapable of feeling anything but pride. In her face was the expression of one whose wishes for her children would be stronger than their own wishes, and the misery suffered by them would be in this woman already suffered. Her hair was a light chestnut color, blond when the sun hit it, and her pale skin held a silkiness like powder. She had plaited her hair in long braids and rolled them in a crown on top of her head, as she did on special occasions. The image of her was the way children liked to remember their mothers, or grandmothers, keeping the hair and face the same in their minds even after old age had grayed both hair and skin. But Sara had not had children to remember her in that way. She had one child, Jesse, and she waited for him now.

She lifted two small shells from the sill, then leaned to pull the covers of the bed into place. She put the pillows on the folded-back edge and covered them with a clean white-ribbed bedspread, knifing her hand with one quick thrust in a way that made the fringe hang at the floor as if it had been trimmed there. She sat, not noticing her expert work but thinking of the tornado a few years ago, and how no one mentioned it anymore, except as a reference in time ("Back before the tornado," they'd say). She thought of how that day had started out bright and clear, with no hint of what was to come.

She glanced around the room to see if it looked right. The sheets had been dried in the sunshine, and she loved the way the room smelled. She had placed some of Jesse's favorite toys on top of the chest of drawers. He would be home soon, for the weekend, and Sara would be ready. I've been ready for a month, she thought. She stood up and wondered how long she would live, sometimes thinking her life would go on forever. She was thirty-three. All her family had lived past eighty. It seemed long enough. The sun came in full across her face, and she looked into it, her heart as open as a blouse.

On the day of the tornado there had been a picnic. The Mount Calvary Baptist Church had grounds big enough for a town picnic and they offered their space each year, just as long as nobody actually went inside the church. Sara had looked forward to the picnic that year. She climbed the hill to the church, a long, sloping hill she had climbed many times as a child, knowing all its ridges and gullies and changes that were almost imperceptible. At first she walked slowly and deliberately, but as she climbed she gained speed, until the grain of land ran smooth beneath her and she seemed pulled by strings that would carry her to the top. Jesse was ten, but he had never seen his mother running, and

called to her. But she did not hear him. When she reached the
top of the hill, she motioned to Jesse and his friends and they ran
too, letting the ground move beneath them. The strings that had
pulled Sara pulled them and they reached the top laughing and
shoving each other.

It was the last Saturday in May and the picnic included
everyone from the town. The morning was pale and white and
people wandered the grounds as if it were a place they had never
seen before. They scattered to swim in the pond and in the
streams that ran deeper in the woods. The younger children
searched for treasures to take home, to put on the windowsill
and during the winter to say this was from the Mount Calvary
picnic last year, or two years ago. There was no warning of what
would happen until the picnic was almost over and Jesse returned with a goat he had brought from a field. People were
packing up their blankets and tablecloths. Some were eating
pieces of cold chicken or cake that had been left out.

Voices from the lake carried over the water. They were children's voices mostly, laughter and squeals and dramatic calls
for help. As the sky developed a greenish cast, the sense of play
quickly folded. There was a stillness that made the old people
afraid. Sara could see a dark cloud reach straight down to the
earth, a finger pointing, moving with a low, bold hum toward the
Mount Calvary Baptist Church. Birdsongs turned frantic, de-
claring a territory they sensed was in danger.

Some children broke a window in the basement of the
church, pleased at being able to perform mischief with the permission of their parents, but not finding it as much fun as they
had thought. They crawled though and unlocked the back door

for the others. The crowd of picnic people surged toward the church like a body of water washing over the land, and Jesse pulled the goat with a steady urging.

"You can't take that goat in there," Bob-Tom said. Robert Thomas was Jesse's best friend. They went fishing together and hunting in the fall. Even before Jesse's fever (the fever that would keep him a child), his friend came to play with him. And as they grew older and the other children stopped coming to Jesse's house, Bob-Tom treated him much the same, making allowances for him with a patience that made Sara marvel.

"Yes I can." Jesse pulled away from his friend, pointing toward the church, then dropped his arm and felt the point was made.

Jesse had wandered off earlier in the day, drawn by the low sound of a bell. He found some goats in a pasture, and when the goats nibbled at his shirt and the pockets of his pants, he took it as a sign of affection. Mary Lil found him chasing the goats. She was exactly Jesse's age and two inches taller. Mary Lil had always paid attention to Jesse, though her attentions were never very kind.

"Coax them, Jesse," she told him. "If you want them to come to you, you'll have to stop chasing them around like that." But Jesse did not trust Mary Lil, so he kept chasing the goats, and the bleating sounds they made, and the sound of the bells bouncing against their necks.

He called to the goats over and over, calling them "kids," even though they were obviously full-grown. It was something he remembered from before the fever, Sara had said, because he never went anyplace that had goats since that train trip through Georgia. He was three, and saw goats being herded onto one of the cars hooked to another train. When they stopped, the animals walked underneath the windows. The smell was so strong that people would not get off the train to get their box lunches, which were already paid for. So the conductor got off and brought lunches onto the train. He had to squeeze past Jesse, who stood on the bottom step of the platform, reaching to touch one of the goats. Jesse answered their bleating noise with a noise of his own. When he went back to his seat, his mother opened the sack and spread out his lunch. She told him the baby goats were called kids.

"Jesse." His friend called to him again, but Jesse pulled the goat by its collar and bell, continuing to walk with a stubbornness that could outdo anything Bob-Tom might try. "It stinks, Jesse. Don't you smell it?"

"Leave him alone." Mary Lil suddenly defended Jesse. It would be something she could talk about later on: Jesse bringing a goat into the church during a storm. Years from now she could say, "Remember that time Jesse brought a goat into the Mount Calvary Baptist Church?" and everyone could laugh.

Jesse's father, Franklin, urged them to hurry. He gestured with his arms. They ran at dead speed, with Jesse pulling the goat and Bob-Tom pulling Jesse. Sara had been walking toward the trees, calling, when she saw them coming across the field. She thought they looked like a scene on her grandfather's Greek coin.

Almost everyone was in the church now and the wind began

to lash against the trees, making them jerk and twist. The goat would not go down the basement steps, and it was plain that Jesse would not go in without the animal, so Franklin lifted the back legs and Bob-Tom lifted the front and they swooped the goat, bleating as hard as it could, into the air, Jesse laughing and loving the noise he heard the animal make.

The hum moved closer now, moved into the heads of the people and into the songs of the birds. Both noises seemed to come from invisible sources, and entered the people, giving them something akin to a sense of rest, making them want to close their eyes.

The door slammed and the wind hit the church like a hatchet, crashing and lifting the pews and altar, rattling the stained glass before it broke, hurling huge pieces of furniture through the walls, picking up the piano and dropping it through the floor. The steeple of the church broke off like an icicle in the hand of a child. Mary Lil was badly hurt that day, so that she never laughed at the idea of a goat in the church basement. Bob-Tom was killed instantly when a small hunk of metal from a windowpane hit exactly at his left temple and lodged in his brain.

The farmer who had owned the goats was killed. His wife had found her husband and son in a pile of rubbish that had been their house. The house was dropped two miles down the road. Sara's house lost half its roof, and all the windows were broken. The tree beside her house, which provided shade for the front porch, was uprooted. And the crops in one of Franklin's fields had been destroyed, as if the hook of a primitive plow had dug one huge furrow.

Sara's leg was broken when a table fell on her, and Franklin had a few cuts, but Jesse and his goat were unharmed. The tornado had somehow linked them together so that when the wind died down, Jesse said he would take the goat home and there was no objection; whereas if there had not been a tornado and Jesse had suggested that he keep the goat, his mother would have said no. For that, at least, Jesse was grateful.

Graveside services were held the next day. Jesse went and stood beside Bob-Tom's casket to watch it lowered. Sara told him that Bob-Tom was to be buried, but Jesse did not believe his friend was in that box, and he was not sad. In fact, he searched the crowd for his friend's face and voice. The people around him kept a cold, hard look of resignation until after the final prayer, when they jerked toward each other and began to scratch their arms, as if they had just awakened.

Weeks later, when Jesse missed Bob-Tom's visits, he locked himself in his room. Sara brought meals to him, to let him grieve. After the third day he walked out before breakfast and took the goat with him. They went to the Mount Calvary Baptist Church, which was still strewn over the field and pond, and he watched the people who had been working there every day, his neighbors, rebuilding, gathering what they could. And there was even some laughter and joking among the men as they worked.

Jesse stayed all day to watch.

That was three years ago. Some trees still lay on their sides where they had fallen. The white maple behind Tinner's Grocery was almost completely soft and rotten because it fell in the marshy land that led to the lake; but Mason, Tennessee, was filled with white maples and poplars and old sweet gums. The tornado had not taken them all.

Sara leaned with her elbows on the sink and watched the up-rooted tree, its torn face lifted from the ground in a way that made her want to weep. The farmers who had cleared their land for crops, but left one tree or two to shade the house, felt a personal loss when the tornado took their only screen from the road, exposing the house and yard to passersby (strangers who could wince or point or look without comment).

At the side of Sara's house, outside the kitchen, branches lay broken and splitting away from the trunk, beginning to have small holes where rain and insects had dug their way in. The roots lay frayed, turned toward the kitchen window, no longer bent to search for ground but dried and curled inward. Sara had seen the wind barely touching its branches when she was a girl and the tree was young. She remembered her father propping it up with stakes and rope to make it grow straight.

When the wind finally had its way, she did not want to have the tree carted off for firewood. She let it lie, trying for three years to think of how to prop it up again, to put stakes around it and the rope, knowing all the time that the roots would not catch hold. She came to accept it the same way she accepted Jesse. The doctors explained how the damage to nerve endings in the brain could not be repaired, and she imagined the tiny fibers curled in and looking as burned and dry as those roots in the yard.

She heard a car drive up and saw Jesse's face framed by the window. Jesse had lived at the Children's Home for six months before returning to spend the weekend with his parents. He had never been away from them, and when Sara saw him coming in the door this morning she thought he looked old, older than herself, older than anyone she knew. Jesse paused inside the doorway before he entered, his mouth beginning to form slow words.

"Nobody came to meet me at the station," he said, his voice almost chiding. But the woman who brought him home corrected him.

"You didn't ride the train, Jesse. I brought you home. I said you could ride the train next time." She turned and pointed to the blue car in the driveway. The woman's name was Miss Harris, and she had orange hair.

Sara held out her arms to Jesse as he crossed the room. She wanted to tell him that she would meet him at the station. His body bent slightly and made him look as if he were always leaning forward. She put her head against his hair and felt his heartbeat through her apron.

"He has grown up in the last few months, hasn't he?" Miss Harris did not know what to say at homecomings. She would leave Jesse at home for the weekend, then pick him up on Sunday night. She would not linger but felt the need to say something. "These pants you sent are already too short." She pointed to Jesse's ankles, and Sara watched the boy smile at his accomplishment of growth.

"He looks wonderful. Just wonderful," Sara said, and she meant it.

Jesse's hair was brushed away from his face in a way that gave him a fierce look. His eyes darted about like a bird's. He was aware of every noise and movement around him, but not their meanings. Sara wasn't bothered by his nervousness but watched him as if not to miss anything he might do. She would save the memories of this visit so that she might bring them out on summer days when no one was home and the afternoons were long. She stored his gestures like a squirrel with its nuts for the winter, and feasted on them over the stove, or sitting at the table, or lying in bed.

Franklin came home early for lunch. When Sara heard him, she straightened her dress at the waistline and pointed to Jesse to stand up. He had entered manhood this year, at thirteen. There were enough hairs on his lip to tease about, he could wear his father's shoes. Franklin almost shook his hand but hugged him instead. Jesse pointed to his ankles and the length of his pants, proud of his growth. Though his mind had not developed beyond that of a four-year-old, Franklin assured him of his height.

Jesse sat back down at the table where he was playing with a dump truck filled with logs. He hauled them to different corners, unloading then loading them again. His movements were slow and calculated and appeared to be due to a meticulous personality.

Sara turned the chicken she was frying in an unconscious manner, knowing when it was done by the amount of sizzle she heard. They could hear Franklin outside, washing his hands and face in the spigot.

"Clear that stuff off now, Jesse, and set the table." Sara handed him utensils, three plates, and napkins. Jesse stood for a moment gathering his thoughts, then moved to his own place at the table and slid the knife down as if he were putting it into a slot. Sara had spent three months teaching Jesse this simple task, and there were times when he did not get it right. Today, though, he put each piece in its correct place and received praise from his father.

"All through?" Sara leaned to lift the hot biscuits from the oven. Franklin sat down while Jesse set the places and Sara brought lunch to them in big bowls. She had meant the question for Jesse, but Franklin answered.

"Not yet," he said. "We have some stumps to pull out." He piled Jesse's plate full of food and spooned Sara's gravy over most of it. This was what Jesse liked. Franklin looked at the trucks his son had parked beside the table, and suggested to Sara that Jesse go to the field with him in the afternoon. And for the first time this suggestion was met with silence. "He'll be fine," Franklin said. "He needs to work." As he talked, he patted his wife's hand. It was decided.

Jesse was four when he became ill. At first they thought it was the flu, but his fever ran high one night, and when they took him to the hospital the doctors told them he had encephalitis, as if they should know what that meant. But they didn't. Not until a week later when an intern explained to them what their life would be like from now on, how Jesse would be regarded as a child but expected to behave as an adult—how eventually he should be placed in an institution. Sara asked the doctor questions, but Franklin left the room.

When Sara called him at home later, he told her he was taking a trip. "Where are you going?" Sara asked. Franklin told her that Jesse was his son, and she said she knew that. Then he told her to forgive him, and that he would be back. He suggested that his sister come to stay with her, but Sara refused. She stayed at the hospital until Jesse was able to return home. Franklin left that morning and was gone three weeks.

It was the end of April and barely light when Sara got home. She took Jesse to the porch and settled him on her lap in the big cushioned rocker. His legs hung over her arm and the arm of the rocker, and his cheek nestled to her bosom with a tiredness she had never seen in him but that she guessed would always be there now. She rocked him and sang songs he had liked before, not knowing if he remembered anything about that time but singing them anyway until his eyes closed and his mouth lay open. The smell of sickness was still on his breath.

Sara watched the sun go down and darkness creep across the field. She would not think about Franklin or where he might be; instead she chose to fill her mind with the field and cars going by in some great hurry to be somewhere. She wondered about the families in those cars, wondered if they were leaving or going home, wondered if they had someone like Jesse.

Louise had held Sara on this porch, had played games with her and rocked her in the same chair. Louise was a black woman Sara had known as a child. She had a lap as soft as pillows, from which Sara could see a wide, smooth forehead and eyes that grew bright with thoughts, and a mouth that spoke the truth. "Let's play the marble game," Louise said, and she made up the rules as she went along. Even then, Sara knew that Louise loved the feel of the cool marbles in her hand more than she loved the game. She placed a marble against her cheek and told Sara, "They're pure glass. All the way through. So you don't have to worry about breaking it. It just chips off; it don't break." She stared into the marble as if she doubted her own words. "There's nothing you can do to break it." But Sara had broken one one time. Split it down the middle, a clean break that had not shattered either piece. She kept one piece on top of her bureau and gave the other one to Louise.

When night came Sara could no longer see the families in their cars, but she heard the swishing noise of the tires. It had begun to rain. And not knowing if it was a man or a woman at the wheel, she pretended she held her baby, that it was four years ago and Jesse was new, his tight face screwed up like a bud that was now calm and open. His hands, which once had grasped and pulled, lay flat. He would never experience a burden but handed that burden in full to his mother. There was Franklin, she thought, but he wasn't there.

When she woke, it was morning and the sun streamed across the porch and hit her face like a bucket of water. Jesse still slept. Sara stretched her legs in front of her to get out the stiffness, and thought about how to order her life.

When Franklin returned, he found Sara and the boy in the kitchen. Sara saw him turn down the driveway in the red pickup she had not seen in three weeks. She did not turn around when he walked in and kissed the back of her head.

"Are you hungry?" she asked.

"No."

"I hired those new field hands you talked to." Her voice

was businesslike before she turned to look at him. "They're out there now clearing the old Fennel place." Sara saw that the lines around his mouth had deepened, and wondered if her own mouth looked as old.

"Fine." He leaned to kiss her cheek. "I'm sorry," he said. His sandy hair and bony face made him appear ethereal, and when Sara turned to him she knew that was all he could say.

"He's a good boy." She led her husband over to where Jesse sat. The boy pushed blocks around the floor, not building anything. He looked to his father, without recognizing him, then turned back to his blocks.

Franklin put on his work clothes and his hat and went to the field. It was spring and he would begin planting.

After one of Sara's lunches everyone felt full and heavy. Jesse took some scraps outside to the goat, which was not penned up but left to roam free in the backyard. The goat's name was Kid, and Jesse had wanted to take it to the Children's Home, but pets weren't allowed; so Sara promised to take care of Kid while he was gone, and when the goat died four years later she would replace it. Through the years she replaced the goats as needed, keeping the same name for each one. Jesse knew when there was a new goat and checked carefully to find a distinguishing mark so he would not be fooled when a new one appeared. Each goat connected him to a time before the fever. As he grew older he knew he was different, but that knowledge could be relieved in the sound the goat made. Sara saw him turn to the animal with a quizzical expression, and she wondered if he saw his other life. The expression lasted only a second, a look of near-recognition, but it lasted long enough to make him cling to the animal more than to anything else.

He enjoyed each goat without mourning the loss of the others. Sometimes he asked his father where they were, and Franklin said they died of old age, for a goat.

Sara knew Franklin had stopped hoping for miracles. Tonight he would take Jesse frog gigging at sunset—Jesse jabbing at the frogs, then letting them go. They liked the frog gigging and those times just before dark when they stood beside the lake and watched the sun go down. But tonight a summer rain came. Huge drops crackled against the ground and onto their shoulders as they ran. Franklin put his arm around Jesse and told him not to be afraid. But Jesse was never afraid.

The rain had stopped when Sara saw them coming toward the house. They arrived soaking wet, and she could hear their laughter. As they came closer, rain clung to their faces like drops of oil. They shed their clothes and Sara brought towels to them. The hour would be late before they stopped talking and playing games. Sara could hear the thunder grumbling in the distance, and the water dripping from the leaves gave an ending effect to the day that eased their minds.

Sara awoke early the next morning. Sometimes she would hear a child's voice call her, a voice that rang clear. She leapt from the bed and would be halfway across the room before she realized it wasn't Jesse. This morning Jesse went off with the goat. He planned to work in the field again today, even though it was Sunday. She went to the kitchen window, where she saw life coming and going, and watched her days begin and end, and knew the weather. She leaned against the sink and let the breeze that always blew come in against her face and lift the hairs off the back of her neck.

Sara was eighteen when she met Franklin. He was four years older than she and had spent two years in the army at Fort Knox, Kentucky. She had graduated from high school one month before, and worked at Bell's Five and Ten Cent Store. Franklin came into the store for some notebook paper (to write to his girl in Kentucky, he said later); but when he saw Sara he wandered the aisles for thirty minutes, until lunchtime, so he could ask her to go for a hamburger.

They stopped at a drive-in and Franklin ordered the hamburgers, making sure she got what she wanted on hers. Then he took her into the country for a picnic. As Sara rode past the trees and houses she had known all her life, she noticed them differently: as if she were in a town she had never seen before and this man had been her husband for eighteen years, rather than the town being her home and this man a stranger.

He asked questions she had never thought about, and it occurred to her that this man, Franklin P. Holden, knew her better than anyone.

"You married?" Franklin's head jerked with the question.

"No," she answered. "Nobody ever asked."

Franklin squinted, as if he thought men might be asking her to marry them every day, as if back at her house lines of men were already gathering at the neck of her driveway to ask for her hand in marriage. He looked as if he had never seen a face so soft, and Sara thought if she touched his hair her fingers would run through it like the slickest water.

He turned onto a dirt road.

"This is McKennon's place," Sara said. "Do you know this place?"

"No. I just turned."

"He's dead now. But there used to be an old bathtub out here." Sara pointed to the trees as if the bathtub could be in one of them. "Over there, I think." She motioned to a scraggly clump of pines. "It's one of those huge tubs with claw feet and a rim that folds back. I climbed in once. It was deep inside." They got out and walked in the direction of the pines.

"I saw my grandmother sitting in a tub like that when I was little," he said. "She was a big woman, but she looked small in that tub. It looked like it had swallowed her."

Sara laughed and took him to the white porcelain fixture beside the trees. "There it is. Guess they have to leave it there. Guess it's too heavy to move."

Franklin wiped out the leaves and dirt. "Get in," he said, turning to hold her arm as Sara removed her shoes and stepped barefoot into the tub. "Sit down," he coaxed. Franklin climbed over and sat down with her. His arms draped over the fat rim like it was a boat. Sara tucked her skirt beneath her legs.

"I'm going to be buried in one of these things," he said. Sara stared into the woods. Her expression was serious. When Franklin took her hand he began to tremble, and the trembling went through them both.

"I have a girl in Kentucky," he said. Sara didn't speak. "I was going to write to her today. I came to the store to get paper to write to her. Then I saw you." His voice had a finality, as if he had made a decision he did not know he had made yet.

Sara released her hand from his and stretched her arms to both of his shoulders. Her touch was so light he had to look to make sure her hands were there. He rubbed her thighs through her skirt and Sara closed her eyes. That's when he kissed her. That's when his hand touched the place she knew she would let him touch the minute she saw him. He was surprised at the wetness of her pants.

"I'm so wet," she said, an apology she did not need to make.

He stood her up and began to remove her clothes, pulling her skirt down with easiness. He removed his own pants and shirt. He had already removed his socks and shoes before he stepped into the tub.

"Who is the girl?" Sara asked, as she watched him pile her underclothes on top of his beside the tub.

"What girl?" Franklin asked honestly. Sara's body was lean and tan and had a fullness around the calves and hips that Franklin liked. He reached to touch where her hip curved out from the waist.

"Your girl in Kentucky," she said. Sara watched him lean back in the tub.

"A girl I used to know." He pulled her toward him.

Sara smiled and lay beside him in the space he provided. He rolled up his pants and placed them under her head for a pillow.

"I've never done anything like this quite so fast," he said. "I mean, not with anyone like you." Sara almost said, "Me neither," but realized he already knew that, and he had begun to probe with his finger in a way that made her hips grind hard against the cold porcelain tub and when he entered her, at first she thought she might scream, but instead put her mouth on his shoulder. And for years when he entered her, right at the beginning, she felt she would scream; and Franklin said it was because she liked sex, but she said it was because she liked Franklin.

It was late afternoon and Sara sat at the table facing the corral, where a mare and a stallion circled the fence. Franklin had taken Jesse to the field, and Sara waited for Pearl to come for pie and coffee. Pearl had been Sara's friend for fifteen years. The pot gurgled its last sounds when Pearl came in the door without knocking.

"Jesse working in the field?" Pearl asked. She had looked around to the corner where Jesse usually played.

Sara stood. "Yes. Franklin says we shouldn't treat him like a child." She brought the carton of ice cream to the table. "He's almost grown now, you know."

"*I* know," Pearl said. "I didn't know *you* knew." Pearl had children of her own.

Sara smiled at Pearl's directness. "I guess so."

Pearl lifted two bowls from the shelf. "There's a final blow that comes with it," she said.

"It's been coming a long time." As Sara spoke she leaned forward to give each word a certain weight, the way she did when she wanted a listener to understand the full gravity of a situation that was too painful to share, one that involved some kind of failing that went back many years. Maybe the failing involved her own family as a child and was carried into adulthood, even affecting relationships with others for years. Until in old age she would understand that the burden need not have been carried that long, need not have affected her life to such a degree. So it would be tossed off at age seventy or eighty, but not completely.

Sara shook her head and scooped a ball of ice cream onto two pieces of pie Pearl had cut. Pearl brought coffee to the table in large mugs. Both women chewed slowly, and turned to watch the horses.

The mare nudged the stallion's nose, moving toward and away alternately. As she backed herself up to him, he climbed onto her haunches. The women did not speak. This was a ritual they had seen before. The stallion moved himself into position until he was no longer awkward, then he pushed with a grace that made the women envy the mare. The mare stood still except for her head that rose and fell with small, high cries, her feet lightly pawing the ground. The hooves of the stallion held tightly to her sides and kept him above her as she backed up closer. When they were through, the great penis of the stallion sheathed itself and the women dropped their heads.

"She sure got hers today," said Pearl.

Sara laughed. "She'll foal within the year." She picked at her pie with a fork. "She's a good mare. She's the third generation since we came to this farm. Before we got married, I brought Franklin out to see this place, to decide if he wanted to live in this house where I was born. He said, 'Why, honey, this is the land of Goshen. We can do anything with this land.' And we have, we've done good." She turned toward the horses. "He brought that mare's grandmama out the next day. It was a fine beginning." The mare circled the fence again, the stallion followed. In a moment they would hear the small cries of pain or joy, they didn't know which.

When the tractor pulled into the driveway, Sara heard Jesse laughing with the men. Franklin told him to go in and clean up because Miss Harris would come by soon. Pearl told Sara good-bye and went out to speak to Jesse.

Jesse came in holding a ten-dollar bill to show his mother.

"Looks like you earned yourself a full day's pay," she said. Jesse's eyes shone, she knew he was happy. "After your shower, come to the porch. I've fixed a chocolate cake for you."

"Okay," he said.

Sara heard the shower running for a long time before Jesse finally emerged fresh in the clothes she had laid out. He stood before his mother. He asked if he could sit on her lap, and as she looked at the size of his body she almost said no. But noticing his face, how it asked to be held, she brushed her lap and patted a place for him, as she had done when he was younger. The sky was almost dark and the orange-haired woman would arrive soon. Sara wondered if Jesse was held by anyone anymore. She guessed not, but tonight she would hold him. She thought of the night when she returned from the hospital, seeing the families in their cars.

There would be sixteen years left in Jesse's life, before he died of pneumonia. Sara would be almost fifty. She would walk into the hospital room and hear the gasps made, and see the nurses holding the oxygen mask a little way from his mouth, like they could not decide whether to hook it back onto his face. She would touch his hands already heavy with death.

"Is he dead?" she would ask, the nurses nodding their heads. The strangles in Jesse's throat pulled at his body, and Sara recognized these sounds as a last effort.

She would telephone Franklin.

"Franklin?" He already knew. "Jesse died just now."

"Were you with him?"

"Yes." Sara tried to think of what he wanted to know. "There wasn't any pain," she said, without knowing if that was true.

"That's good." He said this twice and sounded relieved.

"He went easy," Sara added. "It was easy."

Franklin's voice grew stiff when he said he would be right there and would she wait.

Sara hung up the phone and went to the window to see the dogwood blooming. Both nurses had left the room. Her eyes were as dry as sand. Jesse lay behind her, three feet away, underneath the white hospital bedspread.

In a moment the head nurse came in. She did not speak to Sara but walked around the bed and pulled the cover away from Jesse's face. And Sara saw for the first time the weight of death upon the softest flesh. His mouth lay open as if he were making some hideous noise that no one could hear but would be forever heard by Sara. And she thought again of the goat.

Sara held Jesse in her lap and looked across the field where a hawk circled high, but as she watched, it came lower. "Hawks circle and circle before they land," Louise had told her. "Why?" Sara asked. "To be sure. He's got to be sure of what he wants." Louise had smiled at Sara's confusion. "Come here." She took Sara's small hand in hers. They walked toward a pasture not far from the house. Three hawks circled low, diving toward some bushes.

Louise pushed away the limbs until Sara saw a clearing and a dog, or what was left of a dog. The hawks had picked its bones almost clean, and the clear bright sun beat down and scorched the skin that was left, so that it peeled away from the bones, burnt and dry. The dog had a fierce look, as if at any moment it might rise and attack them both.

Sara jumped backward and the old woman clasped her hand tighter to make her stay, as if she had something to teach that might be helpful later on. "It's all right, honey, that dog can't do you no harm." They did not walk any closer but stayed in the protection of the bushes. "Now, them hawks. They's the ones you got to fear." They watched the birds with enormous wing-spans diving and leaving with bits of dried flesh in their mouths. "They's the ones," she said again, and the tone of her voice made Sara turn.

The old woman watched the hawks, while Sara had not been able to take her eyes off the dog. "Whose dog is that?" Sara asked. She still had hold of Louise's hand, and the old woman moved her thumb in slow circles inside the girl's palm, like if her thumb had been a wing and her body had been smaller, she could have circled with the same kind of ease the hawk had.

"They moves like a song," she said. She had not heard Sara's question. "They moves like a song was lifting them and letting them fall, like they had nothing to do with it themselves; but just somebody singing somewhere could keep them in the air and when that song was through somebody else would sing and that song would keep them up just as good. And it don't matter which song, just as long as somebody is singing." Then she sang something Sara had never heard before, and when she was through turned to Sara, and Sara sang the Doxology.

Sara sang the Doxology now, sitting on the porch with Jesse's legs hanging down the side of the rocker, and watching the hawk almost too high to see.

The Last Fourth Grade

1

I know almost nothing about prisons, but I know enough to hold my glance at the level of an inmate's eyes, and to keep my expression absent of pity. I know how to look straight at people, with no judgment. I learned this particular sensitivity in the fourth-grade class of Mrs. Natalie Johnson. She instructed us to look people in the eye, especially if they were poor or had some misshapen feature. She said it was unkind not to do so. But Mrs. Johnson is an inmate in the Virginia Prison for Women. I have come to visit her, bringing books and a long loaf of bread, and I have been told that I will be escorted to a room with tables, a pot of tea, and privacy.

The blunt hedge around the prison is cut like the work of a cheap barber. Cut by someone who cares nothing about hedges, but who is aware of an effect that comes across as neat, and with an obvious order. Scraggly bushes grow in the dirt beside the office door entrance. I must go through the office into a part of the building where doors close behind me.

The walls hold a burnt smell, or worse, a smell that tries to be clean—disinfectant and old stone. This particular prison has the smell of a school, and I wonder if Mrs. Johnson notices the similar odor.

I am thirty-one, and until a few days ago I had not heard from Mrs. Johnson. Then I received a note asking me to visit her here. I don't know how she knew I had moved back into town, and I wonder if she has thought of me through the years. I have thought about her often.

2

In the fourth grade I wrote a poem about the death of my father, and read it at Writing Time. After class, Mrs. Johnson walked to my desk at the back of the room and told me my poem was good. "Very nice," she whispered. She asked if she could have a copy for herself. I said I didn't mind. She smelled like talcum powder and soap.

That night I copied the poem in a careful, neat hand. I gave it to her the next morning. She thanked me and asked how my mother liked reading it.

"Fine," I said, though I had not shown the poem to my mother.

3

I went to the trial of Mrs. Johnson, and even testified on her behalf. Many of my classmates told the court that she was a good teacher, and that they loved her. I told the judge that she was the best teacher I'd ever had. After the guilty verdict, Mrs. Johnson left the courtroom, a policeman on either side, and I tried to think of ways to rescue her. While she was in prison, I sent postcards. I sent them until I graduated from high school.

At the trial, her arms and legs grew spindly, and as the factual account asserted itself in the newspapers, Natalie Johnson's stout figure changed into a bent, stooped oldness that reached beyond her years. She turned sixty the year she went to prison—only a few years before she would have retired from Vena Wilburn Elementary School.

During the months of the trial, I drew maps, and pretended to be doing this for Mrs. Johnson, as if she had assigned it. Mrs. Johnson loved maps. She pulled them down like a shade over the blackboard and made us see the roads, the mountains, the dark and light terrain of different countries. She pointed out cities and rural areas, then told stories about people who lived in odd parts of the world.

We never knew if the stories she told were made-up or true, but her teaching gave us a way to move inside the maps. She made the lines and boundaries come alive. She traced with her finger, and let us trace with our fingers, the routes that led to historical discovery, or wars that brought life-and-death boundaries to our minds. She said, as she let the large map roll back up above the blackboard, "I love maps. I love all kinds of maps." She let us draw maps of America and color them, drawing in states and boundaries, shading the mountains and making rivers wide and blue.

Before the year was up, every fourth grader felt the contagious affection she had for maps. At recess we drew rivers and mountains and shapes of countries on one another's arms or backs. We wore maps, and drew them, and believed in their importance to our understanding of geography and history.

I also collected luna moths and pinned them to a board. I pretended this, too, had been homework assigned by Mrs. Johnson. I kept trying to picture the way Mr. Johnson might have looked before he died.

4

Natalie Johnson brought students into her home twice a year. In the fall she entertained us the week before Christmas vacation with popcorn and cider; in the springtime, around Easter, she served cookies or cake, with lemonade and ice cream. Her husband, Harry, read the class fantastic stories: fairy tales or tales that scared us into laughter. Everyone called Mr. Johnson "Harry," though Mrs. Johnson was always "Mrs. Johnson."

Harry Johnson had a clear melodic voice and he spent days before our visit choosing stories he thought we would like. Sometimes he made up a story himself. Mrs. Johnson felt proud of her husband and bragged about how much fun he was. She said she had loved him since she was a little girl not much older than we were. She said she had loved him forever, but she blushed when she said it.

Before being promoted into Mrs. Johnson's fourth-grade class, everyone knew they would have a special time at her house—in the fall, and again in the spring. As years went on, though, and as Harry grew older, his stories took on a slightly risqué tone. The year before I was in fourth grade a few of the stories had been categorized as too bold for young ears, and in places even suggestive.

At our first party in the fall, after one of these more bawdy stories, Mrs. Johnson mentioned to her husband the inappropriateness of the subject matter, and we thought we were about to hear our teacher have a fight with her husband. "You're too prim," he told her, and left the house. Mrs. Johnson looked helpless and teary. At the trial she testified to these facts. And as she spoke about Harry, she began to cry, saying she had only wanted him to be more careful about choosing the stories.

The day after our fall visit, Mrs. Johnson read to us a story about Arabian nights. She wanted us to forget about Harry. But many of us had already told our parents about Harry Johnson, and though the parents whispered to one another, no one took action. Natalie Johnson was beloved, she was trusted. Almost everyone in town had been her fourth-grade student.

A few months passed and the class was wondering if the spring party would be canceled. Their parents told them not to mention a party but to let Mrs. Johnson decide. During the last week in March, she sent permission notes to our homes, and our parents signed them.

My mother said she would pick me up at five-thirty and take me to Denny's. Daylight saving time had not yet begun, so the light died around five. She told me to wait outside on the steps.

She knew that in the past Harry Johnson sometimes drove children home in his big van.

5

When we arrived, Harry was in his reading chair and had pillows propped all around the room where children could sit or lean back. He looked happy and suggested that we go to the kitchen and bring our food back to the living room. We loved eating in the Johnsons' living room, because we couldn't eat in our living rooms at home.

When Harry introduced himself, Jeffrey Bohm said, "We already know you. We met you before Christmas." He sounded rude when he said it.

"Of course you did," said Harry. "I remember you." Then he told Jeffrey something that Jeffrey had wanted for Christmas, so Jeffrey would know he remembered.

Harry's eyes were sweaty, watery, and his face slightly flushed, but he was smiling. Still, I was glad I would not ride in the van with him and asked my friend Mary Alice if she wanted to ride with me and my mama to Denny's.

"I can't," said Mary Alice. "I have to go home the way my note says to—in the van."

Harry Johnson urged Mary Alice to sit near him. He said she had pretty hair and that he liked to touch it. "It feels like silk," he said. Mary Alice smiled, and I wished he had said those words about my hair. Mary Alice already had a father who said nice things to her, and my father had been dead a year. I was thinking of another poem I could write, about how much my father loved my hair, when Harry told us to sit down. Mrs. Johnson said she would bring more lemonade and cake in a little while. Ice cream would come last. We always had two stories, but when the second story was told we got ice cream.

The first story was about a frog, and a princess who was looking for a prince. When the beautiful princess kissed the frog everyone made sniveling noises, then Harry stopped the story to ask if anyone had ever been kissed, and when four people raised their hands he said, "Mary Alice, what about you?" And she said, "No, just my parents." So Harry told us, "Maybe before this day is over *everybody* can be kissed." Then Mrs. Johnson came in and he finished the story, but I don't think she heard him ask those questions. She was just bringing in the ice cream.

As he began the second story we could hear her washing dishes. We could hear her rattling glasses and plates, so Harry called out for her to close the kitchen door because some of us couldn't hear with all that noise. But no one was having trouble hearing. When she closed the door, Harry scooted down on the floor with us, near me and Mary Alice, and he pulled Mary Alice onto his lap. I had never seen anyone drunk except on TV, but I knew that Mr. Johnson was acting strange.

Mary Alice looked at me. Her eyes scanned the room to see reactions, but Harry said, "Now I'm going to hold Mary Alice on my lap and I'm going to put her into what's called an armlock. Some of you boys know what this is because you've seen wrestling on TV." The boys nodded, but we still didn't know what was happening.

Jeffrey Bohm said, "Let me do it. *I* can do it."

Mr. Johnson spoke roughly. "Now, Jeffrey, sit down and

watch how Mary Alice tries to get loose." Mary Alice wiggled trying to get out of Mr. Johnson's arms, and her wiggling made his eyes shine. He held her tighter.

"Hey, no fair," said Jeffrey. "You're holding her too tight. That's not fair." Others seemed to be frightened, because Mary Alice herself looked as if she were about to cry. Her bottom lip quivered. So he let Mary Alice go and said, "Okay, Jeff-boy, come over here and we'll see how you do."

Jeffrey took a position on his hands and knees, as a wrestler would. "This is how it's *supposed* to be," he said.

I could see a bulge in Mr. Johnson's pants, and his eyes looked glazed. He was looking at me. He even reached to pull me onto his lap, but I slipped out of his grasp and followed Mary Alice into the bathroom. "I hate him," said Mary Alice. "I want to go home."

"I do too," I said.

"When your mama comes I'm going with you."

We heard some scuffling and someone yelled. When Mary Alice and I came out of the bathroom, Jeffrey was standing up hitting Mr. Johnson in the head. Harry Johnson was kneeling, holding on to Jeffrey's pants. He wouldn't let go. Mrs. Johnson stood at the kitchen door. "Harry! What are you doing!"

Harry sat back on the floor. His pants now looked wet. Mrs. Johnson gathered us up like chickens, and we hurried into the kitchen. She blocked the kitchen door with a chair and then turned to us. "I'm sorry. I shouldn't've brought you here today. Mr. Johnson, he isn't well. He's sick, I think he's sick." She kept her voice very calm, so we began to feel calm within ourselves. She said we could take a walk and she would show us some bird's nests, maybe an owl, and if we walked all the way to the pond we could see some funny-looking fish.

Jeffrey clung to Mrs. Johnson, and Mary Alice and I walked along beside him. Jeffrey could not stop trembling, and Mrs. Johnson comforted him every few seconds. Her voice sounded deep, as from a cave. "Don't you worry, Jeffrey. You are just fine now. Don't you worry." She stroked his head and back. "You didn't do anything wrong, and Mrs. Johnson won't take you back there again."

I tried to comfort Mary Alice in the same way, my hand on her back.

On the way to Denny's my mother asked us about the party and said how nice Mrs. Johnson was to invite us to her house. She said that since the Johnsons never had any children of their own, they thought of the fourth grade as their special children. "They must like having young voices in that stuffy old house." My mother pulled into the Denny's parking lot.

"It's not stuffy," I said, in defense of my teacher.

6

A few days after this incident, Harry Johnson was found dead in the backyard of his house. At her trial Mrs. Johnson claimed that he had shot himself. She said he hadn't meant to but was cleaning his gun and it went off. She looked at the jury, people she knew, people who knew Harry, and she tried to make an excuse for him. "He probably didn't know what he was doing. He was so drunk. During that last year, seems he was always drunk."

But what happened, Mrs. Johnson finally confessed, was that she had come from teaching one afternoon and found Harry with pictures on the kitchen table: photographs of children in underwear or nude. His camera was on the table beside her car keys, and when she came in, though she barely remembered the exact moment, she would see forever the vacant, stupid expression on his face.

Natalie Johnson took the gun from in their hall cabinet, and she shot Harry in the chest. She could not stand to be around him. She could no longer bear the thought of him in her house, or alive. Until that moment, she had not known she was as capable of murder as she was of love. She said all these words at the trial, and I remembered her words, the way I remembered about maps and countries.

Harry had been shot three times.

Mrs. Johnson confessed, "I shot him, then shot him again. I don't know how many times." She tried to stand in the witness chair, but the prosecutor laid a hand on her shoulder. "I didn't know what else to do," she said. "I couldn't hear those sweet voices in the schoolroom without thinking of Harry."

She hated him with her whole heart.

7

Mrs. Johnson's letter asking me to visit her in prison said: *I know you probably have not thought about me in many years, but I remember you. I remember everyone in that last fourth-grade class from the year Harry died.*

I had thought about her often, and had thought about visiting her in prison. I didn't know what I could say, so I dropped the idea. I couldn't imagine what she wanted to say to me now, but I decided to go. I wanted to see her.

She was sitting in a large room with windows. Her hair was thin and very white. She had lost weight, but she didn't look as gaunt as I had expected. Her face looked pale from lack of sunlight.

"I'm Carey Hammond," I said, using my maiden name.

She raised one arm and started to rise.

"Well, it's Bowles now, though I'm probably going to be Hammond again soon. I divorced my husband a month ago, and moved back here."

She asked me about my husband, my life. She was hungry for news.

As I drew closer, I couldn't help seeing the hardness that had crept into her face, the lines and rough skin that had replaced her plump, soft body. I wondered if she still smelled like powder, like Chanel No. 5, which we all knew was her favorite perfume.

"I have a daughter," I told her. "She's nine."

"She must be in the fourth grade." Mrs. Johnson smiled. "Does she live with you?"

"She's with me during the week but goes to her father on weekends."

"Oh, I was hoping you might bring her by." Mrs. Johnson looked embarrassed at the suggestion. "I guess that wouldn't be appropriate," she explained, "but I'd love to see her. Does she look like you? You were such a thin, wiry child."

"I'll bring a picture next time," I said. "Maybe I'll even bring Soskia."

"Soskia?"

"My husband's family is from Czechoslovakia." I thought of the shape and boundaries of that country as I said it.

We sat at a small table near a window, where someone had placed two cups and some tea, with Ritz crackers on a paper plate.

"I have some jam in my room, but I forgot to bring it." She called her cell a "room," and I was surprised that she could keep food there. I must have looked surprised.

"I'm a teacher here at the prison," Mrs. Johnson said. "I teach reading and writing to women who never learned, or who didn't do so well in school. Sometimes I teach geography, maps." She smiled. "I get special privileges because I help to rehabilitate. I don't know who I am unless I'm teaching." She chuckled, so I did too. I was glad I had come by.

"I want to tell you something," she said. Her hands grew nervous, her fingers wiggling like worms. "Since I've been in this place, I've thought a lot about Harry, and what he did. And you might be surprised to know that I realize now what really happened." She turned to look at me. I couldn't read her mood.

"Harry was a good man until the year of that last fourth grade," she said.

"Yes, ma'am," I said, falling into an old student habit of polite agreement.

"Sometimes I believe Harry is still in the house, sitting in his chair," she said sadly. "And I write poems to him—the way you did to your father. I still have that poem you wrote for your father. Did you know that?"

"No, ma'am." I felt that I had been jerked up, then let down again softly.

She removed her glasses and squeezed with her thumb and finger the bridge of her nose. She put her glasses back on. "Would you like for me to show you *my* poems sometime?"

I nodded without giving consent.

8

I had felt closer to my father after his death than when he was alive. The poems I wrote made me feel close to him. When he was alive, he traveled on business most of the week, so my mother and I seemed to live alone. In fact, Mary Alice thought my parents were divorced. "He's gone all the time," Mary Alice said. "Why is he gone all the time?"

"That's his job. He has to go. But when he's home, he's real nice." And he was. On the nights he was home, he tucked me in bed, and I felt that the house was safe in a way I never felt when he was traveling. He brought presents from places like Ohio and Washington and Texas and he showed me those places on a map in my room. We put pins in the map so I could see where he would be going the next week, and I liked it better if the states were close-by. He called us every night, usually just before bedtime, and asked me something about my homework. Sometimes he told me to memorize a poem so that when he got home I could say it to him. He liked when I knew something by heart.

So when the car he was driving crashed into another car, and my mother told me he would not be coming home, and that we would be going to his funeral, I wrote poem after poem, hoping he would see that everything I was writing was "by heart." And when I wrote them down, I felt he was alive, and near me. I never showed anyone those poems, except one I showed to Mrs. Johnson.

9

Soskia could hardly wait to see my fourth-grade teacher.

"Is she old?" she kept asking. She had dressed in her best Sunday outfit, and I tried to tell her that the place we were going was a prison and that it wouldn't look like other buildings where she had been. I told her that people were locked up because they had done something they weren't supposed to do, and Soskia asked what my teacher had done. I said that I would explain when she was a little older.

"When I'm ten?" Soskia asked.

"Older than ten," I told her.

The day was gray with a light drizzle, and the prison appeared especially dreary. I tried to distract Soskia with gifts we had brought for Mrs. Johnson. I gave instructions about politeness. "Don't mention Mrs. Johnson's clothes," I said, "because in prison you have to wear an orange outfit. Everybody has to wear the same thing."

"Why?"

"They just do. It's a rule."

"Will she like my dress? Will she think it's pretty?"

"Yes."

Soskia turned as we went into a section where doors closed behind us with a metal lock. We walked toward the room where Mrs. Johnson waited. She had put on a sweater over her orange clothes, and she looked almost normal, sitting at the table with some tea and a plate of crackers. I had brought some snacks to put out. Soskia seemed shy when she saw Mrs. Johnson, but she wasn't shy for long.

"Soskia." Mrs. Johnson said the name with immediate affection. "Look how dressed up you are. I feel like we're about to have a party."

Soskia grinned and sat in the chair that Mrs. Johnson had pulled out for her. I asked Soskia if she wanted to open the bag and offer Mrs. Johnson one of the cinnamon buns we had brought. We put out food, and Mrs. Johnson spoke in tones that made the moment seem celebratory. Soskia began to tell Mrs. Johnson about her dog—a puppy—and how it liked to chew up shoes. She told her the puppy's name and said she had gotten it just a few days ago. She said we couldn't stay long, because we had to get back to the puppy.

Mrs. Johnson knew all the right questions to ask. Then she told Soskia that she had been my teacher many years ago. "And I remember when your mother was the same age as you are now." Soskia looked at me as though Mrs. Johnson might be teasing, so I nodded and said it was true.

"My daddy doesn't live with us anymore." Soskia's face looked quite thoughtful. "He lives in Maryland, and I go to see him on weekends. Mama says he can't live with us in the house anymore."

"Well." Mrs. Johnson buttoned her sweater, then lifted a piece of paper from her pocket. "Maybe I should show you this." She unfolded the paper to reveal large block handwriting on unlined paper. The lines were crooked and went down the page in a diagonal. I recognized it as the poem I had written to my father.

"Sometimes," said Mrs. Johnson, "if somebody in the family is gone, or not in the house"—she made the situation sound regular—"people, especially children, find it a good idea to write something to that person. Even if you don't give it to them. You can write a poem or draw a picture, then when you see the person again, if you want to, you can give it to him. Or you can put it in an envelope and mail it. If you want, I can help, so you can surprise your daddy."

Soskia surged forward with excitement. She wanted to begin that very moment. Mrs. Johnson obliged by asking the guard for paper and a pencil. In moments she was leaning over Soskia, guiding her hand across the page. I watched, remembering the smell of talcum powder and soap. My poem lay open on the table, and I could see the blocky letters and the lines that went down in a slant.

10

We visited Mrs. Johnson every Sunday for six months. She never again brought up the subject of Harry. Still, I felt uneasy, without knowing the source of my uneasiness. One Sunday, Soskia got home late from an afternoon with her father, so that our visit was whittled down to only thirty minutes. That was the day Mrs. Johnson looked angry as we walked into the visitors' room.

"Well," she said. "Glad you could come." She moved to pull out something from a book bag she carried. "I wanted you to see some pictures of Harry. Soskia has never seen my Harry."

"Who's Harry?" Soskia asked.

"He was my husband." Then she paused, holding her mouth

tight, pursing it. "Your *mother* remembers him. Don't you remember him?" She looked hard at me. "Your mother *liked* him." I had never seen the particular face she showed to us now, this odd expression. I almost didn't recognize her.

"No." I spoke defensively. "I liked *you*, not him. At the trial, I spoke for *you*."

"That's not what I mean, dear," she said. "I mean you and Mary Alice, all you little girls—you wanted to make Harry pay attention to you." Her hands were folding and unfolding a ratty piece of paper. "You know what you did."

I asked Soskia to go to find a nurse. We called the people who worked in the prison "nurses."

"Mrs. Johnson, what's wrong?" I said. "Why are you doing this?"

"You and Mary Alice, some of the others, too, you had your flirty ways, your teasing girly voices."

"What are you talking about? Are you saying we *wanted* Harry to do what he did?" I couldn't believe Mrs. Johnson had lived so long with this idea. "You think we *wanted* him to touch us?"

Mrs. Johnson had become unglued. She wasn't listening to me. "Your sweet-smelling hair," she said. She put down the piece of paper and began to wring her hands, as if she were washing them. "And you sat with your little dresses open, legs sprawled out like *whores*. You let him see your little-girlness. What was he supposed to do? He couldn't help himself." She spread the pictures of Harry on the table. "I should never have brought you into the house."

I stood up, wanting to leave. "But you *did* bring us there. You put us in the room with him." I was furious and rushed toward the door, so I didn't see the moment her face changed, but I heard the sound she made, like a breath-cry. When I turned around to say one more thing, her face was buried in her arms.

Her voice came out muffled, full of tears. "I *closed* that kitchen door," she said. "I closed that door and washed my dishes, making noise so I couldn't hear. I didn't *want* to hear. I was *glad* when he told me to close that door." She looked up, her face wet. "I stood at the sink, and washed and washed, then I heard Jeffrey yelling." She paused, then looked straight at me. "As long as everyone was quiet, as long as there wasn't any noise, just Harry's story-voice, I could keep on washing. But when Jeffrey started to yell, I had to come through the door and see."

She strained to get up, pushing on the sides of the chair. She almost fell, and I caught her, helped her to stand. "He never touched you, Carey, did he? Did he?"

"Don't talk," I said.

"I thought he was getting better," she continued. "I thought it might help to have children in the house. He always wanted children of our own, you know." Her eyes grew huge, and she looked at me without actually seeing. "Then when I found the photographs, then I had to do what I did, you see. He never would have stopped."

"Don't," I said, reaching for her arm.

"Mama?" Soskia stood at the door. I didn't know how much she had heard, or how much she understood. She hadn't gone for a nurse.

"Soskia! Go!"

Mrs. Johnson was still talking, not yelling but speaking in a soft, singsong voice. I tried to comfort her.

"Don't say anything nice to me," she said. "That door has been in my mind, and now I've opened it. I know what I was thinking while I washed all those little plates and dried them, taking a *long* time. I think part of me thought that if Harry got caught, if he went far enough to get caught, *then* he would stop. Then he would stop. I wanted to save my Harry."

"We're all right," I told her. "The whole fourth grade came out all right. Mary Alice is a lawyer, and Jeffrey owns a large business in Richmond. Everyone in that last fourth grade came out all right."

"Well," she said, but her eyes had changed color. They had turned black, completely pupils. I felt that I could see all the way to the bowels of her soul. She sat down again, as if she had fallen into her chair. Something seemed over, and in a few days I would realize that what was over was her own life.

On Thursday morning when the guard came to Mrs. Johnson's "room," she was found dead on her cot. She had died of a heart attack during the night. The warden asked if I could come identify the body. Not knowing whom to call, they called me. When I arrived, I found Soskia's pictures and writing taped to the wall over her bed.

11

The weeks are long without her.

Soskia and I went to the funeral with a town full of old fourth graders. Now, on Sundays, we sit and talk about her. I didn't tell anyone about the door Mrs. Johnson's words opened in *me*. I didn't say how I had envied the attention Mr. Johnson paid to Mary Alice, how I had wanted that attention for myself. I didn't tell how Harry Johnson met me at the door that day, how he slipped his hand beneath my dress and rubbed my back and bottom, my legs. I was aware of pleasure I had not felt before, though I knew this was a wrong kind of pleasure. He had lifted me up and whispered something in my ear that I didn't understand, so I laughed and touched his cheek. For one moment, I felt like he was a father, though not mine. Mine was dead. I could see Mrs. Johnson standing behind him, smiling a false, hard smile. She put her hand on his shoulder, and he put me down.

Yesterday, Soskia mentioned that she could still bring back the smell of Mrs. Johnson, and asked if she was "remembering the smell, or was Mrs. Johnson really close-by." I told her I thought she was close-by. I told her that sometimes a teacher is so strongly imprinted on our minds that we carry that teacher with us through the years. Soskia asked what I remembered when I thought about Mrs. Johnson.

"That's easy," I said. "I learned about maps and far-off countries. Maybe I even married your dad because of what she taught me about other places. She kept my father alive for me when I needed him." "What about you?" I asked. "How do you remember her?"

Soskia took my question seriously, "Well, I think about how weird she was the last time I saw her. But mostly, I remember how she taught me to draw, you know, pushing my hand over the page until I could feel how to do it myself. But what I think about most is the way she would hum in my ear. She hummed real quiet while I was trying to do something, and when she did that, hummed, I could do it right."

"The humming," I said. "I had forgotten."

"And now, when I have to do something real hard, and if I think I can't do it"—Soskia looked out over the yard—"I hum to myself, so quiet my ear can hardly hear the sound—and it's like a little road I go on, that takes me straight to the top. And I can do anything."

Natalie Johnson had taught her fledglings with a hum. I myself had forgotten. With a steady sound she had borne us like water toward the sea, her head wide with secrets. Her last fourth grader was Soskia: art lessons, writing, maps. Boundaries Mrs. Johnson herself could not keep. Harry and his hands rose like wings beneath little dresses, and Mrs. Johnson swept her house clean.

Snail Darter

In the middle of a hollowed-out room, a man leaned to remember being carried somewhere. Not carried on a horse. He didn't remember that. But he remembered being carried in someone's arms and then on a train, though at the time he didn't think of it as being a train. He only knew it now, when he was older and could stand at the train station, waiting. He didn't wait for anything or to go anywhere, but stood, then sat, looking up to the huge space above him. He loved the sooty smell. He loved to hear the steady clacking of wheels when the train came in, see the deep steamy burst of air when it stopped. And he thought of the man who brought him here.

His first trip on the train began one day in the spring forty-seven years ago. He was six and came to this town in Tennessee after recovering from an illness. His body had recovered sufficiently, but his mind stayed locked and he had the stare not of a regular six-year-old but of someone who was bored or pre-occupied.

He had had a fever. When his mother gave him laudanum to help him sleep, she forgot she had already given him a dose and so gave him a second one. It was enough to put him into a deep, limp sleep that almost took him.

The doctor arrived to see the boy's stillness and ordered a horse to be saddled. He asked for three heavy belts. The mother did as she was told. Dr. Sam Parham was not the only doctor in town, but he was the one everyone trusted the most. He placed the child in front of him on the horse and wrapped two of the large belts around them both, strapping the child to his own chest and waist. The child's head bent downward. They galloped off.

The mother, who had not asked anything until now, called after the doctor, "Where are you going?" but they did not go anywhere. They rode back and forth in front of the farmhouse to jog the child awake. The doctor rode hard for hours, and even when it began to rain he didn't stop, letting the rain sting their faces. The mother watched from the window. The father was not around.

They ran like that all night. The horse's mouth frothed, but the doctor would not stop or rest, nor did he allow the horse to rest. Toward the end, before morning, the horse's gallop turned measured and slow. So the doctor hit the horse with the third belt, on the high brown haunches, hitting and hitting, because the child had begun to stir, to make noises, groans; but the horse was not able to give more running. The doctor's bladed belt pushed down the hooves into the soft earth, then raised them again, the effort giving the effect of speed. But the speed had slowed, so that the child was barely jogged now. When morning broke, the horse died.

And if someone had been watching (the mother at the window slumped asleep, her other children asleep), if someone had been there to see in those furious moments before morning, they would have felt the mindless life of the horse move into the boy, awaken him, giving only one way out of that black hollow where they had spent the night. And they would have heard the doctor shouting, and the horse's hooves steady against the slow earth, and above all, the labored breathing sounds.

The child had already opened his eyes, waking only slightly, never coming all the way back. The doctor carried the boy into the house, the boy as light as shadow. And the families who had given their children laudanum when they were sick no longer kept that medicine in their houses.

The doctor took the boy to live with him, appealing to the courts to allow it. The mother, a thin, furtive woman with a house full of children she couldn't care for, did not protest but let it happen the way the doctor wanted. The day they left town, the boy carried a satchel as thin as paper, the other children played in the yard, and the mother stood with her back to them as she stirred something boiling on the stove. She waved with the flat of her hand, but the doctor knew when they drove off that she stood again at the window. When the child called for his mother, the doctor patted his knee or his shoulder, or kept his hand on the boy's head. He told the child that he was his uncle, and over the years it was an easy lie for the boy to believe.

The spring day they arrived in Sweetwater, Tennessee, a

downpour caught them as they walked between the train and the station house. The boy, who loved the rain more than he loved the sunshine, said, "Stand, stand," which meant he wanted to stand in the rain. The doctor urged him inside the station house with the promise of candy or a balloon. But he couldn't offer anything as fine as rain.

The doctor enrolled the boy in school and he was promoted through grades along with his age level. Each year the difference became more apparent. Children would ask him his name, and when Oliver said "Oliver Brise," it came out garbled and sounded like "Abba." The children laughed and called him Abba all through grade school.

"Abba means 'father' in Hebrew," his uncle told him, trying to cheer him, give him pride in a name the children chose in cruelty. But Oliver liked the name and didn't feel the cruelty, not in that, at least. The cruelty Oliver bore was in the exclusion he felt.

"Abba. Abba has his pants on backwards," one boy yelled during the middle of a history lesson. They were in the ninth grade.

"Abba is fine." The teacher called him Abba too. She knew he had never worn his pants wrong, and the others knew too. The only one who doubted was Oliver, who looked down to see if he had done everything right—zipped, buckled, everything. He was never sure.

He knew one girl, Edith Setler. She was not the prettiest girl in school, but she wasn't the ugliest either. Edith walked him home from school; sometimes she sat beside him at lunch so that other girls began to do the same. The boys started to invite Oliver to join their games. Oliver was never happier than in that ninth-grade year. The next year he took a job at the drugstore or around town, where they still spoke to him and sometimes asked him to sit down. Oliver joined them, but he knew not to stay too long.

The year Edith was a senior, Oliver saw her walking home from school and called to her. She stopped, stood for a moment, as though she couldn't think of his name. Then she said, "Oliver," and they walked along together. He had just taken a job as paperboy. Edith asked him about it.

"It's good." Oliver's head stiffened with the effort to sound normal.

"How's your uncle?"

"He's fine." He looked to the books Edith carried and frowned at the signs and symbols on one.

"Trigonometry," Edith told him. He tried to repeat the word but couldn't. "And it's sure not easy." She rolled her eyes in a way she used to, to indicate difficulty. Oliver laughed.

"Not easy," he said, and took hold of Edith's hand.

Oliver had grown to be six feet two inches tall. He was not good-looking but didn't have a distorted look. His eyes were particularly large and held that same blankness they had always had. "Edith," he said, not knowing what he would do next, not even knowing what he wanted to do, except that he had wanted for all these years to hold her hand. But now, as he did, a larger impulse swept over him and he pulled her against him, her books hitting against his chest and stomach and her head bumping his chin. She dropped her books and ran from him.

Oliver stood at the corner and saw her move away, her blue dress flying up around her knees and thighs, her arms moving out beside her as if for balance. When she turned and saw he was not chasing her, she stopped and stood for what seemed to Oliver a long while. Then she called to him. Oliver didn't answer. He stooped to pick up her books and looked up once to see if she still stood there. His face was red with an embarrassment he didn't understand. A storekeeper saw the incident and came out, but he saw Oliver picking up the books and didn't see anything wrong. Others stood at the windows of shops to watch what Edith would do. She returned to where Oliver was. He handed her books to her, her papers stacked neatly on top.

Before Edith took the books she put her hand on his shoulder, and Oliver's mind went suddenly to the loss of his mother that day and the doctor's touch on his shoulder, knee, and head. He felt comforted.

"I'm sorry," said Edith. Oliver nodded and said it was okay. She took the books from him and told him she'd see him tomorrow.

Oliver continued down the street in the same direction as Edith, knowing that he had moved from a confusion that felt devastating to a confusion that felt good. Edith's blue dress swished as she walked, and he showed his gratefulness to her from that time on by merely waving to her from far off. But sometimes when he passed her house, she might come out and they would talk and she would ask how he was.

Oliver couldn't remember the name of the town he was born in. He only knew that Sweetwater was his home, though sometimes he made trips to other towns with his uncle. He knew too, though vaguely, of a ride long ago on a horse and how the horse died as Oliver himself had lived through that night. He knew of the spurious courage of that night and the doctor's decision to take him away from his home. Oliver had been told the story, so that his remembering came more from the telling than from memory. And each time he was told, he knew that the horse's death meant both his own life and his own doom, though he couldn't say how he knew this. And he knew that moving to Sweetwater with his uncle had somehow saved his life.

One year before his uncle died, there was an uproar around Tennessee which involved the building of the Tellico Dam and a small fish, two and a half inches long, called the snail darter. The dam's configuration blocked the fish from reaching the spawning ground upstream, and unless they were relocated the chance of their becoming extinct was almost assured. It was thought at that time that Sweetwater, Tennessee, was the only place left where the snail darter could survive, and the building of the dam was stopped by order of the Supreme Court. Oliver's uncle followed the story and told it to Oliver, who loved the idea that people would stop the building of a dam to find a new home for the fish. Biologists came to Tennessee to designate a seventeen-mile stretch of shallow water as a critical habitat. But at the same time there were Cherokee Indians who were also affected by the building of the dam. The water would flood more than twenty of their sacred villages, including the village of Tanasi, which had become the name of the state. The doctor crusaded for both the Indians and the snail darter and found an irony in the attention given to the two-and-a-half-inch fish.

Everyone talked about the snail darter and how it stopped the building of the Tellico Dam, and the doctor liked to tell

Oliver how they, too, had been relocated, brought to Sweetwater, the water they would live in.

Oliver was almost seven when Mrs. Constant came to work for them. She had no trouble with the boy and was even able to control him when he flew into one of his tantrums.

"Constant," he yelled, "bring Abba a comb." But Mrs. Constant would not do everything Oliver wanted.

"You can get the comb yourself, Oliver dear," she would say. And after a stubborn, silent refusal or else a demanding Indian-like yell, Oliver got up to get the comb himself. Sometimes he threw it at her, sometimes he combed his hair in front of the mirror, then messed it up with his hands, pulling it straight up so that he looked as if he were floating underwater.

Mrs. Constant would take the comb and fix his hair, neatly parting and smoothing down the sides. She ignored him when he ran his fingers through it to undo what she had done. The doctor praised her patience, her ability to hold her temper.

Once when Oliver threw the comb, he was standing very close to Mrs. Constant, so that the comb hit hard on the side of her nose. She reached and slapped his cheek, and though this did not surprise Oliver, the doctor had to leave the room to keep from interfering. He noted the next day that there was still a faint patch of red on the boy's cheek, but Oliver seemed to have forgotten.

The way Oliver remembered that block of time—the year or two when he spent his nonschool hours with Mrs. Constant—was this: he remembered her large body, which seemed to him like some huge rock, and he remembered when she had to stay with him at night because the doctor was gone. He remembered how she screamed at him when he couldn't sleep, or if he woke with a nightmare and called out. He could still see, sometimes at night, her big, stocky, fat-legged figure bursting into his room, so that he must have cried out or made some noise or shout that brought her, because she came at him, appearing suddenly. And she seemed to be in flight, a huge bird that hung over him. He could even hear small birdlike sounds that came not from her mouth but from her throat, as she filled the night with her consternations. And it seemed to Oliver at those times that there were more people there, more than just this bird woman who descended and hovered above him whenever he cried out and woke her from sleep.

"I'll teach you," she cried. Her voice had the quality of a hissing goose. "You broke my sleep." Her red hair flew in all directions, her breath rank with a smell Oliver couldn't identify. She hit Oliver. Her fists, at first, lay closed and hard against his head, then her fingers opened to scratch him, make him bleed. Sometimes she lifted something from the floor and used it. If the thing she chose was heavy, Oliver would be knocked unconscious. Oliver didn't know why she came in to him during those nights but thought, as children do, that it was surely his fault and that he would be glad when the hitting stopped, as it always did.

Oliver's mind wanted only to fall asleep, quiet and sleep. When she left and he watched her go back down the hallway, a lassitude settled on him, made him unable even to cover himself. Rarely did she come back twice in one night. Some nights, though, she would not come in at all, and when Oliver woke and saw the dawn he knew he had slept through and had not suffered her hands. And he always believed on those mornings that these terrible nights were over.

It was on a January night that it ended. His uncle always arrived home earlier than expected. Oliver heard the car drive up and tried to mention it to Mrs. Constant.

"Constant. Constant."

But Mrs. Constant yelled her drunken talk, saying much that made no sense to anyone but herself. And Oliver was always surprised how the next morning she would be sitting at the kitchen table with toast and jelly, offering to fix eggs any way he wanted. But at night all he saw was her stoutness coming toward him against the hall light, her fists ready.

His uncle was in the room by the time she had hit him twice. He threw her against the far wall, startling her into a fit of short rage, then crying, then pleading.

Oliver watched dumbly. He watched his uncle, or the man he now called his uncle, yell at this woman to get out, get out, *get out*. His face raged in the same way hers had, only this time not at him. Oliver, relieved to have the protection, had not expected it or even thought to ask for it.

Mrs. Constant left. They never saw her again. The doctor looked over Oliver's body to find bruises, cuts the woman had made. Some of the cuts were already healed. He stayed near the boy until sunup, not sleeping but staying to cradle Oliver. The boy slept, though fitfully. And when he woke with his inevitable nightmares, the doctor was there to say, "It's okay. Okay, Oliver," saying it over and over again, like a chant. "Go back to sleep. I'm

here. I'm here." And he would brush the boy's hair from his forehead with one hand.

It was past sunup when the doctor himself went to sleep.

There was a space of about ten years when Oliver wore a blue
serge suit. He wore it both summer and winter, though in winter
he wore a heavy coat over it. The suit grew shiny and people
began to mention to his uncle that he should have a new one. But
Oliver didn't want new clothes. Finally, someone gave him a
soldier's coat, medals still on it, captain's bars intact. They gave
him two pair of gray pants to go with it. For a while Oliver wore
only the pants and the jacket he had worn before. But his uncle
saw him try on the coat in front of the long hall mirror, walking
back and forth, saluting. Then one day he wore it into town. He
saluted everyone, making the gesture a little high with fingers
pointing upward, as the British do. No one corrected him, but
returned the salute and began to call him Soldier. He liked the
name.

Soldier ran all his years in Sweetwater, ran as smooth as he
could. He took jobs his uncle found for him, and when his uncle
died he took from the town. Now his face grows rounded and
more aged, not aging as quickly as his body. His eyes stay young,
though, and so does the way he walks or rides his bike.

Some days he sits at the train station and watches the one
train come and go. He sits on the steps of the trains parked in the
stalls, but mostly he sits inside the station house. People think he
remembers his early train ride and that that longing brings him
here, but he isn't reminded of anything exactly, he only returns
to sit at a familiar place.

But there are moments when he seems to remember, when his body moves into a position. He turns his head as though he has heard something and just been caught in a snapshot. And at those times, when he listens, gives all his attention, his back sits straight, not slumped. He is a picture already taken, his head held with an abrupt dignity, like that of a servant who feels proud in his work.

But all the while something works inside him. He sees his mother at the stove, lifting only the flat of her hand when he left, and Soldier holds his own two hands together.

He spends his life marveling (without knowing he has marveled) at what he has lost. He wonders where his life is, feeling at some point it was shifted. He wants to be carried somewhere. So he leans into the dark smell of the station house and finds comfort in the high-ceilinged room, the black glint of long, narrow track. He finds comfort in strangers who speak or nod. But he could no more say what that comfort was than he could say what makes him feel lonely or tired.

Sometimes he says out loud, not to anyone, but out loud, "Please, don't make me remember that."

Biology

In April the All-Churches Revival came to town.

The revival came every year, held in a tent on the fair-grounds outside Mercy's city limits. People came from all around Georgia, some from as far as Jefferson or Athens, to hear the preacher who had led these meetings for nineteen years. I had never been to a revival before, because my family didn't become religious until my daddy left home. But this year a young man replaced the older one. His name was Warner James, and when I saw his picture on the posters, I knew I wanted to go. He was handsome, even his name was handsome. People who knew him called him Warn, and he said that's what he was here to do: warn us.

His face on the poster enchanted me, and at fifteen I wanted to be enchanted by men. I had already been courted for a year by Lowell Hardison. Lowell took me into the fields and gave me long, hard kisses. He said he loved me and meant it. I said I loved him, but he was not deceived. I could not deceive him any more than I could deceive a tree.

Lowell had shown me how to carry myself. He taught me to walk around naked in the shadows. But whenever he touched me, he was always in a hurry. Lowell was two years older, and he never took his slow sweet time.

My mother and a friend of hers went with me to the first night's revival. Her friend was a man, and even though my father had been gone for five years, I didn't like to see her with another man. I wanted to take Janey Louise with me to the first night, but even though Janey Louise lived in our house, and her mother, Volusia, was our maid, they could not do many of the things we could do, because they were colored.

The tent was huge. The top swayed down in loops like a circus tent, and a million chairs must have been set side by side, facing the preacher.

Warner James stood at the podium, talking to people and waving everybody in. He urged them through the microphone to sit down front, and whatever he said sounded personal. His voice was like a movie star's voice, and I felt caught by the timbre of it.

When the invitation came to give yourself to Christ, he loosened his tie and a shock of hair fell down onto his forehead. His voice boomed with the fact of God's love, and people began to walk up front. I felt moved to follow them. I wanted to have God's love in my own heart.

Warner James noticed me immediately and came over to hand me a small white pamphlet. He took me to some chairs, away from the other saved people, and suggested we sit down.

He looked at me the way men look when they think I'm pretty. He took my hand, and I could see a wedge of hair that stuck above the top button of his shirt. He asked if I wanted to stay and help them prepare for the next night's meeting. I said yes.

After everyone left and the tent was empty, Warner James asked if I had ever been saved before.

"No. I never even came to a revival before. But I do go to church sometimes."

He moved his chair up close to mine, and I could smell his aftershave. He talked to me softly about Eternal Life and the soul. He said that he could see my spirit and that my spirit was strong and full of the Lord. I felt like bursting open when he talked, and could not take my eyes off his face and the small tuft that poked from his shirt. His hand brushed lightly on my arm, and he touched my hair once to push it out of my eyes.

"You're a very pretty young lady," he said to me. "Did anybody ever tell you that?" I could not remember, at the moment, if anyone had ever said such a thing.

"I don't think so," I said. He was thin and lanky in the way of my father, so I told him that August (my father's first name) had gone to the Sea of Cortez, and then I told him I had been there. I made my life sound privileged. He listened to all my words with a quiet attention that made me feel interesting and important to him. I couldn't believe the excitement I felt. Finally, he asked if I could come back the following night.

"I'll be preaching here for a week," he said. "I'd like to see you again." He acted as if he had asked me for a date.

"I can come tomorrow night," I said. "I planned to anyway."

"Well, plan to stay a little later." My heart leapt up. "Wait until everyone has left and we'll have some refreshment in my trailer. It's parked over in the woods." He pointed to a spray of trees, and though I couldn't see the trailer, I said, "Okay."

He stood, and as we left each other I kept thinking about the word "refreshment."

When I told Janey Louise, she said, "You better be careful of that man. He's a preacher."

"But he is so handsome. He looks like Jeff Chandler."

"So what?"

Then she told me about a boy named Dake who lived near her school. Seeing him, she said, made her feel excited and tired at the same time. She wondered what it would be like to kiss him.

"Do it!" I said.

The next night I put on some high-heeled shoes and a dress I'd been saving to wear for Lowell. I sat between my mother and Mr. Shallowford, the man she was seeing. I sang hymns and felt saved. When Reverend James called people to come forward, when he made the invitation to dedicate our lives, I could watch others struggling with their souls. I felt proud and full of the Lord's love.

When the call was issued, Warner James looked at me with his bright blue eyes and I nodded only slightly to let him know that I had remembered to come back. I'd thought of nothing else all day. I'd washed my hair and soaped my body twice. I'd bought a new slip at Kresses, because my own best slip was looking ragged.

I told my mother, "The preacher asked me to help hand out tracts for him tonight. I'll walk home when I'm through."

"Well, isn't that nice," my mother said, turning to Mr. Shallowford. "Evie's going to help Reverend James." She was proud. I had never been interested in God before. "Don't be late," she said.

After the service, after the saved had gone home, Mr. James walked me to his trailer in the stand of trees behind the tent. He opened the door for me, and I was surprised to find how big the trailer looked on the inside. He had a table and chair where he ate, and a sofa with a green velvet cover. He turned on the radio, and music came out from the walls. I felt like I was in a picture show, and said it.

Mr. James laughed and went toward the refrigerator. "I'm going to have something to drink," he said. "Would you like something, Evie?" He had a deep laugh that made everything sound fun.

"I would like a Coke-Cola, thank you," I said, trying to sound older.

He took out two glasses and some ice that he kept in a small, fancy bucket in the freezer. He removed his sport coat and threw it carelessly across a chair.

I didn't want to sit down where he threw his coat, so I moved toward the sofa and sat on the edge of the velvet as he handed me a glass of ice. He poured my drink into the glass without speaking, and everything seemed crazy and from another world. He smelled like cigarettes and cinnamon. He sat beside me and reached gently for my hand.

"I'm glad you were willing to wait and come back here with me." He touched my arm to show how he appreciated me.

I nodded.

"I'm happy to see you. Your dress is so pretty."

I had put on lipstick, applied after the meeting, after my mother and Mr. Shallowford had gone. I did not use my regular Tangee Natural from Kresses but a new Revlon color called Red, Red Rose. He leaned to touch my lips with his lips, just slightly, and I could not speak or breathe.

"I hope that was all right," he said. "I can hardly help myself, you are so lovely."

"Yes," I told him. Lovely. He had said I was lovely.

He stood up to open a window and we could hear the new spring sounds. As I listened I could identify each one, so I named the sounds for him: the chirping sounds of baby birds, a loud bullfrog, wing-sounds of a bat. A nightingale sang. We both heard it.

"That's a nightingale," I said proudly. We heard an owl.

"You're smart as well as pretty. I'm lucky to be with such a delightful young lady."

Delightful. The words he used were strong medicine to my heart. I wanted him to kiss me again, and tried to send a silent message from my mind to his that would make him wild to touch me. He stood up to get another drink for himself.

"Does it bother you that I'm so much older?"

"No. Not at all," I said. "I hardly even notice it."

He laughed and when he leaned down again, he lifted me up with his arms, holding me like a baby. "I want to be close to you, if that's all right. I'm wanting so much to touch you and be close."

"Sure," I said. This was nothing at all like Lowell. Lowell would never take the time to talk this much, and he would definitely not carry me in his arms. I could not believe Mr. James had lifted me. I felt his breath on my ear.

"Mr. James," I said, "I must be heavy for you."

He stopped and let my body slide down, holding me close to him from my head to my toes.

"Now, Evie," he said, "if we're going to hold each other, you'll have to call me Warn, not Mr. James."

"Warn," I said, but it felt like I'd said *Warm*. I *did* feel warm. Hot. I felt my body about to turn into flame. My dress came undone at the waist, and my breasts grew heavy with desire.

He took me into a small closet of a room, with only a bed and a rod where he hung his clothes. He laid me down and looked at me. I could not think of anything to say. He touched my breasts, turning his fingers around on my nipples. They were hard like little pebbles. He kissed me through my dress, and before I knew it, my dress was unbuttoned and he was pulling it off around my knees. He paused at my knees and looked at my slip, its newness. His hand went under my slip and he touched very lightly the crotch of my panties.

"Evie," he said. Just saying my name, then saying it again. "Evie, Evie." He sounded like he was singing. I closed my eyes and let him wander over me with his mouth and hands. I felt so loved. I had never felt so loved. This is what I had wanted all my life, I thought. This is what I've been waiting for. I never wanted to see Lowell again.

The next night I sat again between Mr. Shallowford and my mother. I could hardly wait to end the hymns and the sermon, the invitation, the call of the soul to Eternal Life, then again to follow Reverend James to his place in the trees where he touched me again and our bodies traced each other without speaking, just the language that made me feel alive.

He taught me to kiss his back and arms and legs. He taught me to nibble with my lips like a little fish. Caressing him tiny, tiny times, over and over. He showed me how to use my hands and make him come. But on the third night he said that he would go into me, and I said okay. He knew by then that I was not a virgin, because I had told him about Lowell. He said nothing when I told him. I was afraid he thought I was cheap.

But he decided that night to go into me, and I could hear myself making small cries, as though this wasn't even me. "I love you, Warn," I told him that night. "I love you, I love you." He did not say anything.

My mother was still up when I got in. She sat at the kitchen table talking to Volusia. They looked serious, and I was afraid they knew all about me. But when I came in the door, their mood changed quickly and their voices shifted to a new tone. Finally, my mother spoke.

"Evie, I don't think that preacher should keep you out so late. What are you doing over there?"

"We give out material, and he talks with people who come up front. There were lots of people tonight. I help him clean up a little bit afterwards, and he gives me a Coke-Cola."

"Well, I don't think you need to help him anymore." She stood up, but Volusia watched as I went to the refrigerator and cut a hunk of cheese to take upstairs.

Janey Louise was waiting with the bedroom door open.

"Come *tell* me."

"I love him," I said.

"No, you don't."

"Yes, really. It is so *sad.*"

"What're you gonna do?" she asked. "He'll have to leave in a few days."

"*May*be."

"Whaddaya mean, 'maybe'?" She closed the door to the bathroom so that we were completely closed in. We had wallpapered the doors to match the room, so the doors when closed were not distinguishable except for the knobs and the molding. We felt like we were inside a box.

"Well," I said.

"You're gonna have to forget about that man. What'd he do, anyway?"

I lay back on the bed feeling sexy and older. "He touches me everywhere. He kisses me all over my body, and I kiss him like that too."

"You do?"

"Yes. It's great. I feel shivery just thinking on it. He says it's okay because we are in the lap of God."

"The *lap* of God? What does that mean?"

"It's just God's lap, that's all. You're in it too. And he says he's never seen anybody so full of love as I am. He says he is *glad* to know me."

"Well, maybe he *does* love you, girl. Maybe he's gonna take you away from here. From me. I don't want you to go away."

"I'm not going anywhere. Maybe he could stay here," I told her. "Maybe he could get a church here and he could wait for me. Just live in Mercy till I grow up."

"Whoo."

On the last night of the revival I didn't go to the meeting but waited until my mother had gone to bed, then snuck out to see him. I wanted to tell him my thoughts.

"Warn," I said, still thinking of him as Mr. James, but calling him Warn. "I've been thinking how you might stay in Mercy and get a church around here. Maybe not in Mercy, but close by, so we could keep on seeing each other." I looked straight at him when I said this.

Warner James did not say anything for a full minute. I was afraid he hadn't heard me. Then he said, "Evie, you are a wonderful girl. You should not waste yourself on the likes of me."

"No. I *want* to. I *want* to waste myself."

He took my head and held it like a vise. "Evie, I'm wanting you to do something for me tonight. I'll probably have to leave tomorrow after the service, so I want this last night to be very special for us."

I tried to figure out what he meant. "What do you mean?" I asked.

"I want you to put your mouth on me."

I had heard about this kind of thing, but I was frightened and didn't want to do it. He begged me, and asked if I wouldn't do this one thing for him, since he had brought the Word to me and saved my soul, wouldn't I do this one thing for him?

"Evie, Evie." His hands ran up and down my legs and I let him dismantle me. His fingers went everywhere, and for a while he kept his own clothes on. Then he asked me to undress him. He instructed me slowly, and when I'd taken his last piece of clothing off, I knelt beside him on the bed.

He pulled my head down onto him and I closed my eyes, feeling him rise toward my mouth. He held my hands and I put my lips over him, moving off the bed to slide down between his legs. I was surprised at how good he felt in my mouth, his pulse against my lips and tongue. I felt the power of how good I could make him feel. He moaned and moaned again. I did not want to stop. I moved with him until a new taste surprised me. I sat up and he smiled, but his eyes did not focus, and the way he smiled seemed to have nothing to do with me. I knew that he would be leaving and that not even this last act could make him stay.

"Baby, oh baby." He pulled me back down against him. "Now let me do you." But I moved away. I stood up and moved to the other side of the trailer against the sink. I picked up my clothes and began to put them on. He did not love me. I knew that now, as clearly as if he had said it harshly to me, as if he had yelled it. I dressed and went home, sneaking into the back door of the house and up to my room. Janey Louise waited for me in the dark. She was awake, as she had been every night, but that night she pretended to be asleep. Finally, when I had brushed my teeth and washed and washed my mouth, she said, "What happened?"

"Nothin'."

"You *lie,*" she said. "Something happened."

"Same thing," I said. "Same thing happening every night with that ole preacher."

"I don't see why you going to see him *every night.*"

"He makes me feel good." I turned toward Janey Louise, who faced me from her own bed.

"What's he doing to you?" she asked.

"*You* know."

"But tonight. What'd he do tonight?"

I told her that I put my mouth on him.

"No you didn't."

"I *did*."

"You're a *nasty* thing."

"No I'm not. It was good."

"Would you do it again?"

I turned away, wanting to end the conversation. "He's leaving tomorrow. That's why I did it."

We were quiet awhile. "I've heard of people doing that," she said.

"You have?"

"Yeah. And once I heard my mama talking about it with Joe Sugar."

I could hardly bear to think of Volusia, or of my own mother, doing such a thing. I wondered if my daddy ever asked my mother for that kind of love.

"Oh well," I said. "Let's go on to sleep."

"Evie?"

"What?"

"Will you tell me sometime how to do it?"

"Sure." I felt proud and sinful all at the same time. I felt as though I'd earned something by my act, and I was glad I wouldn't be seeing him again.

The moon was full that night, and though we usually sat at the window or went outside into the yard on the full-moon nights, we did not mention doing so. Later, when I couldn't rest, I sat near the window. Janey Louise's breathing was steady and full of hard sleep. I sat on the floor so the moon could hit my face, the way the sun did in springtime.

Some nights I could crawl into the moon and live for a short time in its reflected light. Private secrets were being kept in the pockets of my robe, and a certain signal from outside, a bugle sound from a new bird, could release my hunger from its hurt world. I wanted to ask someone for food.

The next day I opened the closet where my mother kept August's old clothes. Was she saving them for him? Until a year ago, I could still smell him on the sleeves of his jackets. My mother's clothes were in the closet next to my brother's and mine. A dress that belonged to Volusia and two shirts of Janey Louise's were at the end. One dress hung beside another, and my father's jacket touched a dress and a shirt. Shadows and forms of people being friendly in a way that the real bodies could not.

I kept thinking about the ways I gave my love to people and how they didn't know what it was. I decided not to love anybody for a while, except the moon. I would love the moon, and feel valued by it. I made a decision not to lie down with anyone again until I felt the love I wanted to feel.

I took out some paper and wrote to August. I hadn't written to him in almost a year.

Dear August,

I know you are surprised to hear from me, but I have not gotten a letter from you in a long time either. So I guess we are even. I wanted to tell you that things here are fine. Last week I went to hear a preacher. He was in Mercy for a whole week, and I went every night. I gave my life to Christ.

I believe I know now what I want to be. A teacher. I want to teach

*biology—teach people to look at everything around them, the way you did.
I like my biology teacher, Mrs. Kirby, very much. She has taught us about
spiders and what good architects they are. We spent one whole class period
watching a garden spider spin its web.*

*Mrs. Kirby set the spider on an upright stick with water beneath him,
and he dropped—fast—not by a single thread, but by two. I was amazed.
When he got to the surface of the water (just before he reached it) he
stopped short, and somehow broke off one of the threads. The thread floated
in the air and was so light it moved like a breath. Mrs. Kirby put a pencil
to the end of the thread, but it wouldn't stick, so she let the spider step onto
the pencil and wrap the thread around it until it was taut.*

*Then there was a kind of floor on which the spider went back and
forth. When I see a web now, I cannot tear it down. She is teaching me
more that I will write you about.*

*I am also sad, and miss you very much. The other night I walked to
the front of the revival tent and gave myself to God. But I am thinking now
that I was already God's, wasn't I? Like the spider? The spider can't give
itself to God. All these things are going around and around in my mind,
and I can't tell anyone about it. But I can tell you. If we could start writing
again, I would like it very much. Also, I would like to think that I could
come back to the Sea of Cortez and visit you there. You have not seen me in
a long time.*

Love,
Evie

O Tannenbaum!

Every year Daddy Bert, who was not my father but my uncle, liked to take his whole family into the woods to choose a tree for Christmas. The yearly trek had been a family tradition since Sib was four. Sib turned nineteen this fall, and he was my idol. He was captain of both the football and basketball teams at Whittier High School, and coached my Little League baseball team for two years. More children had been born after Sib: Cal, Bob, and B.J.—but none as good as Sib was on the field or court. The only cousin in that family who was near my exact age was Babe, a girl. Still, I never minded being paired up with Babe when our families got together. Babe was fourteen, good-looking, and she knew how to act like a boy.

During the Christmas season of 1982, my parents decided to get a divorce, and my sister, Julie, and I learned that we were to spend Christmas with Daddy Bert's family. My mother had always bought our tree from the local nursery, so Julie and I envied Babe's exciting trip to the woods. The trip was made even more mysterious by the secretive attitudes of the family. Daddy Bert had never included anyone outside their immediate circle, and though we always ate Christmas dinner with Daddy Bert and my aunt Val, and though I saw the tree each year and thought it looked pretty much like any other tree, still, what actually happened in those woods was something of a secret. Swift glances and nudgings occurred when the tree was mentioned, and Julie and I went wild with curiosity.

When we heard we would spend Christmas with Daddy Bert and Val, Julie asked, "Can me and Will help them get their tree?"

"I'm sure you can," our mother said.

I could hardly wait.

The day before the trek into the woods my mother brought us to Daddy Bert's house. We had shopped for gifts, wrapped them, and while the presents were brought into the house I followed Babe to the backyard. I wanted to make sure we would be included in the trip this year.

"We're going to get the tree tomorrow, aren't we?" I asked.

"Yeah." She giggled. "You're not gonna believe what happens!" she said. "If you go, you have to promise not to say anything about it afterwards."

"I won't," I said, wondering.

"Can you shoot a gun?" she asked. "I mean, how good are you?"

"I'm all right," I said. "I've been hunting with my daddy and some of his friends. Squirrel hunting, doves, and once we went looking for deer. Didn't see anything, and most of the men just got drunk."

"Yeah, well," Babe said. Her hair had grown longer in the last few months, and though it was still brown, it was a lighter brown. Her eyes in the cold December air glowed bright blue. She looked like the picture of somebody in a magazine, but I couldn't think who. I loved to look at her.

"Why're you asking if I can hunt?"

"Not hunt, silly, shoot. I asked if you could shoot a gun."

"But why?"

"You'll see," she said.

My mother called into the back room to say she was leaving and that she would be over for Christmas dinner, but she didn't think my daddy would be coming and maybe I would like to make time to see him on Christmas Day. She gave me his number and new address. I put it into my back jeans pocket and tried not to look sad.

That night I dreamed of Babe, her skin and hair, and I dreamed she was older than she was now but looked the same. I dreamed that she let me touch her and I woke up with a hard-on. This had happened before and sometimes I waited for it to go away, but sometimes I did something pleasurable about it.

The next morning, when I came down for breakfast, I found everyone dressed in warm clothes, ready to go into the woods, except for Bob. Bob was sick, and though he begged to go anyway, Aunt Val wouldn't let him. Sib was discussing whether to take a ladder.

"We haven't needed a ladder in three years," Daddy Bert said. "We won't need one this year either."

"Why a ladder?" I asked.

"You better get dressed, Will, if you want to go with us. Is Julie still asleep?"

I grabbed a muffin from Babe's plate and ran back upstairs. Julie and I were dressed and ready in ten minutes. While we were drinking orange juice, Aunt Val made some toast and wrapped a fried egg inside. In the summer, when we came to Val's, she always made us fried-egg sandwiches for breakfast, frying them in bacon grease. We ate them leaning over our plates.

Daddy Bert came into the kitchen with a gun on his shoulder. Sib carried one too. I didn't say anything and had told Julie not to ask any questions, no matter what she saw. Julie was surprised to see the rifles. She looked at me as if she expected an explanation. Babe looked at me, too, and nodded. She seemed glad I was keeping quiet.

We rode outside town and parked the truck, then walked, spreading out in pairs to search for a tree. B.J. and Cal stayed with me and Julie, guiding us about what to admire but not choosing anything. All the trees that Sib and Daddy Bert liked were eighty feet tall. I tried to point out other trees of a more reasonable height, but no one paid any attention to my selections.

"This one," Babe said, pointing to an enormous tree. She looked all the way to the top. "This is the one."

"I believe it is," Sib said. B.J. and Cal grumbled. They had moved into the teenage attitude of being bored with anything anyone else did or said. They wanted to be somewhere else, where no adults were in sight.

"What d'you think, Will?" Daddy Bert asked. He made me feel included by asking the question.

"It's just so *big*. How can we cut something so big?"

"The trick is this," Sib said. "We don't *cut* it down."

"What?" But before I could get out another word, Daddy Bert had fired the first shot. He was shooting at a spot about six feet from the top of the tree. Sib shot second, then Cal, B.J., and Babe. When they finally handed the gun to me, they told me where to aim and I shot. The treetop creaked and began to tilt downward. As it fell, it crashed through larger branches, then got lodged on a spreading limb. Everyone yelled and made me feel as if I had brought the tree down all by myself.

"It was just the last shot," I said modestly, but still I felt heroic. I was sorry that Julie had not had a chance to shoot.

"Good shot, Will," Daddy Bert said, and everyone congratulated me in turn. Julie came over to where I stood and said, "This is crazy."

The treetop, from what we could tell, was intact. The branches looked full, though a few had broken off. "How big is it?" Cal asked. "Can you tell?"

"Looks to be about five to six foot," Sib said. They were trying to jostle the tree loose.

"We'll have to get a ladder," Babe announced. "I knew we'd need a ladder."

"We passed a house when we turned into the woods," Julie said. "I bet they'd have a ladder."

Daddy Bert told Babe to ride with Sib to get the ladder. "Take Will with you," he said.

We drove about a half mile before we saw the mailbox that said *Arthur Childs*. Beyond the mailbox was a small wood-frame house. We rang the doorbell and a man with a beer belly and a shirt that did not quite cover his stomach answered the door. Sib asked the man if we could borrow a ladder, and the man cut him off in midsentence.

"What in the hell do you take me for?" he said. "Some kind of *fool*? You think I'm gonna give my ladder to three delinquents who come out of the woods and ask for my stuff? What, are y'all on drugs or something?" He turned and yelled, "Jolene! C'mere. C'mere and see these fools."

A woman came to the door and stood behind Childs. She was slight, with bad teeth, and she had been cooking. She was not large but very pregnant, and her apron barely wrapped around her stomach. Her hair was pushed up into an unruly ponytail. The house smelled like grease and cats. The whole scene was like something from a bad movie. Sib asked again.

"Yes ma'am, I just wanted to borrow a ladder," he said, "to try to get something out of a tree. I'll bring it right back."

"What you got up in a tree?" the woman asked. Until she spoke, I hadn't noticed that she was young, probably not many years older than Sib. Childs looked more like a father than a husband.

I could tell that Sib didn't want to explain. "My little brother's caught up in some branches and we need a ladder."

"Oh, Arthur, quit being such a jerk and let them use our ladder. What's the matter with you?"

"You're crazy, Jolene. You'll never see that ladder again."

"Then go with them. Hell, I don't have anything to do, *I'll* go with them." She fumbled with the knot in her apron, laying it over a chair in the living room. Childs went to the barn to get their ladder and settled it across the back of his truck. He tied a red kerchief on the end.

"We'll come with you," he said, satisfied now that these kids would not gyp him out of anything. Babe and I had said nothing, but as we went toward the truck, Babe began to talk to the woman, to ask her questions.

Sib stopped the truck about a fourth of a mile from where Daddy Bert was waiting with the others. "Let's walk in from here," Sib said.

"How far is it?"

"Not far," Babe said. She kept chattering to the woman. Jolene had let Babe touch her stomach, which looked tight as a drum, and Babe jumped when she felt the baby kick. Babe laughed and told me to touch Jolene's stomach, but I didn't want to. Sometimes, I thought, having a girl along was a good thing. A girl could make people feel at ease in ways a man couldn't.

B.J. had climbed up to the first limb, trying to dislodge our Christmas tree. Childs propped up the ladder, and Jolene called to B.J., telling him to be careful.

"Who's that?" B.J. yelled.

"We're gonna get you down, honey," Jolene said, practicing to be a mother.

"You've got to step back." Sib took hold of Jolene's arm to move her out of the way. In that moment, the treetop came loose, a few limbs broke, then it crashed to the ground directly in front of Jolene. As if in response Jolene said, "My God, my water's broke."

For years, I believed the tree had broken her water.

Just the week before, my mother had explained to me and Julie how sometimes love cannot last.

"You *mean* for it to last," she said. "You expect it to go on forever. Then something happens. Life changes the way you feel—the way you are."

"Which one of you did it change?" Julie had asked. My mother looked stunned.

"Both of us," she said defensively.

"But why are you so *mad* at each other?"

"We're not." She turned up her collar in the back. When we didn't argue with her, she relented. "Well, this morning on the phone I was mad, because I couldn't agree with your father about what we should do now."

"You've been mad for years," Julie said, now as angry as they were. I was the only one not mad, and I wasn't sure why.

"I'm not ever going to get married," Julie said, "and if I do, I'm not going to let this happen."

"I hope that's true," my mother said. "I mean, I hope this won't ever happen to you, and that you will stay married forever." We were wrapping presents to take to Daddy Bert's, and my mother handed me some Scotch tape. "Love's a good thing," she said to no one, "if you can keep it."

I taped the packages, and Julie stuck on the bows. As we wrapped the gifts, my mother forced her mood to change. She grew cheerful and put on some Christmas music.

"I know you'll have a nice Christmas with Uncle Bert," she said. Bert was her brother. "And Aunt Val said she would make one of her mincemeat pies. She'll have so many good things to eat."

"Where will *you* be?" I asked.

"Oh, I'll come for Christmas dinner but not Christmas Eve. Her face changed so quickly that her mouth and eyes looked like a mask with deep hollows. She would spend these three days before Christmas by herself.

"Can we call you?"

"Oh, honey," she said. Then, "Of course you can."

I thought of all this as I saw Childs leap toward his wife. They had seemed angry at each other earlier, or at least irritated. Now Childs seemed to feel that if anything happened to Jolene he might die right along with her.

"We've got to get her to the house," he said. "We can call the hospital from there."

Sib and Daddy Bert scrambled to help carry Jolene to the truck. The boys offered to hike back to town to get the doctor, and I noticed that Julie wanted to go with them. Babe and I wanted to stay and see what was going to happen. We walked to the truck behind Daddy Bert.

"Can you drive?" Arthur Childs had turned to me. I couldn't believe he thought I could drive.

"I'm *twelve*," I said.

Sib drove Childs's truck, and Arthur Childs rode in the truck bed, holding Jolene. He had removed his coat and covered her with it. Babe and I rode in the back, and Babe kept stroking Jolene's face. She seemed grateful.

"Don't fret," Jolene whispered.

Cal, B.J., Julie, and Daddy Bert brought the tree in the other truck and followed us to Arthur's house.

We got to the house at five-thirty.

"We'll call the hospital," Daddy Bert said.

"No time," Childs told him. He had been married before, had grown children, and had delivered several of them himself. "But I sure could use your help." The house was small and now smelled like stew. The first little wave of heat that hit my face made me want to touch Babe. I kept wondering what I would be like as a lover.

"The stove's on," Babe said. Jolene could speak, but her voice was low, growly. And every few minutes she let out a groan.

"Arthur," she said. "What am I going to do?"

"Well, honey, you're going to have this baby right on schedule. You'll have it right here." He helped her into the bed and put something beneath her hips to lift them. He told Sib that he needed some hot water and towels.

Then he told me and Babe to boil water.

"Lots of it," he said. He told us to tear up some sheets in the hall closet for rags. He also said to get some liquor from the cabinet in the kitchen. I was glad he let us stay. I felt important in a way that hadn't been part of my life in a while.

We could hear Jolene scream now. She was cursing at Arthur, but his voice stayed calm and low.

"I'm glad I won't ever have to go through *that*," I told Babe.

"I won't mind it," she said. "It's just pain."

"I wouldn't like it." I tore the sheets into towel-size rags. I liked the sound of the cloth tearing.

"Sometimes there's no other way," she said.

We carried the hot water and rags to the room where Childs was tending Jolene. We peeked in, trying to look around Sib and Daddy Bert. "Y'all get out of here," Sib said. He leaned down and whispered, "Why don't you take the tree out and put it in the stand. It's in the back of the truck. Bring it in and decorate it. We'll just give that tree to Mr. Childs and Jolene."

I couldn't believe that Babe and I would get to decorate the tree by ourselves. A box of ornaments was in the corner, along with two strings of lights and a star. We put the tree into the stand, and I held it down while Babe put the star on top. We stood the tree in the corner.

"You have to put the lights on before the tinsel and Christmas balls," I told her, parroting my father.

"I know that," Babe said. She untangled a string of lights and began to wind it around the tree. Extra lights lay in the bottom of the box. We became so engrossed in our decorating that Jolene's yells became a kind of background noise, and we didn't think about her until she stopped suddenly and we heard a baby cry. We had almost finished decorating the tree.

"Gosh," Babe said. "It's born."

"Yeah."

We went to stand outside the door, which was slightly ajar. Sib told us to come in and look at the baby, a tiny, wrinkled creature, flailing its arms and releasing a pitiful cry. When Jolene spoke, she sounded angry.

"Get it out of here," she said. "Make it stop crying."

"It's got to cry, Jolene, honey. That's the way it fills its lungs. It's got to cry to live."

"What's its name?" I asked. No one answered me.

"Is it a boy or a girl?" Babe asked.

"A girl," Childs told us, and I wondered, though he seemed quite content, if he was disappointed.

Jolene kept worrying about the baby's crying. "What's the matter with the baby?" she said. "She sick? Is something wrong with it?"

"She's just perfect, Jolene," Childs said.

"Doesn't she like the baby?" Babe asked.

Then I saw, to my amazement, that the baby was still tied with a blue veiny cord to its mother. The smell of blood and mucus was strong and made me want to vomit. Childs let Sib hold the baby and wound some string around the veiny stem. I yelled when I saw Childs's large, blunt hands lift the scissors and cut it.

"Does that hurt?" I asked no one in particular.

Then Mr. Childs held the baby up for Jolene to see. He looked proud in his chest. "I have four kids," he said, "but I never had a little girl. Look, Jolene. Look at her." He put the baby beside Jolene and reached his big finger into the baby's mouth to pull something out, though I couldn't imagine what that baby would have been eating. Then, while the baby was next to Jolene, he pushed on her stomach hard, and Babe and I both gasped. Something popped out of Jolene. We thought another baby had fallen onto the floor, but it was a sac, filmy with blood.

Jolene told Arthur to get out. She told him to take the baby with him and to get out. "This is not some kind of goddamn show," she said.

"What's the matter?" Sib asked Arthur.

"She's mad," Arthur said, "because I've been through this before and this is her first time. She wants it to be the first time for me too. She thinks it's not special to me." He held the baby like a practiced father. "She doesn't know that every time is a first." He handed Sib the tiny bundle, wrapped in a small blanket I had brought in earlier. "How much you suppose she weighs?" he asked.

Sib held the bundle awkwardly, worrying that he might drop her. "I don't know," he said. "Maybe six pounds?"

The house was getting dark as daylight dwindled, and when the truck drove up with its lights on, and the doctor got out, the kitchen clock struck nine.

The doctor stayed with Jolene for a while, and Arthur asked if anyone wanted something to eat. He asked the doc and Sib too. Babe turned on the stove to reheat the stew. We put bowls and plates around the table. Babe kept saying, "I wonder why she doesn't want that baby?"

When the doctor came out, we heard Jolene yelling at him as she had yelled at Arthur. "Keep that baby away from me till I get some rest." Arthur pleaded with Jolene to let the baby nurse. The doctor took the baby and laid it beside Jolene. Jolene turned her back.

"I'm going to sleep," she said.

The doctor motioned for us to leave the room. "We're going to have some of that good dinner you made, Jolene."

"Add a little more salt if you need it," she said, as they closed the door.

We ate the stew and some vegetables that were almost black with cooking. Sib noticed the tree and Mr. Childs turned and saw it for the first time.

"You kids do that by yourselves?" he asked. His voice didn't seem anything like the man who had answered the door and didn't want to give us his ladder.

After about an hour Jolene came out of the bedroom, walking unsteadily. She looked at the baby wrapped and sleeping in a blanket on the couch. She lifted it and gave the baby her breast. "I guess I'd better do this," she said, without much enthusiasm—though she lifted the baby with tenderness. The baby began to suck, and I was startled by the size of Jolene's breast.

Babe caught me looking. She jumped up from the table and turned on the tree lights, then told me to come outside. I wasn't through eating yet, but I usually did whatever Babe said to do. We ran down the road.

"Where're we going?" I said.

"Keep running."

We ran to a small stone ledge by the road and climbed onto it. We sat in silence for a moment before Babe said, "You know what I like to do?" She scooted closer to me. "I like to look in people's houses at night, when they don't know you're looking. I like it at Christmastime best—to see the different trees and imagine what their lives are like."

The stone wall felt cold beneath my jeans, but I liked sitting there with Babe, looking at the house. We could see the tree lights blinking on and off, and Childs, Sib, Doc, and Daddy Bert around the table. Jolene stood beside the tree with the baby.

"If somebody saw my house right now," I said, "they wouldn't see anything. All the lights would be off. Nobody would be there."

Then Babe turned and kissed me hard on the mouth. I could feel moisture on her lips, could taste it. I tried to kiss her back. I leaned forward to touch her lips again, but she moved away.

"Babe?" I said. "What did you do?"

"I kissed you."

"Why?"

"I thought you needed it. You know, with all that's going on in your family and everything."

"It's all right," I said. "I mean, my parents might get divorced, but we'll be all right. It happens to a lot of people."

"I don't think I could stand it," Babe said. "If Daddy Bert and Mama split up, I couldn't stand it."

"Well, it probably won't ever happen to you." I shifted my weight on the wall. "Babe?"

"Yeah."

"Maybe when we get big, maybe we'll get married."

"We can't, stupid, we're cousins!"

"If you're cousins, does that mean you can't ever get married?"

"Not to each other." She jumped off the ledge. "You think they're in love? I mean, Jolene and Mr. Childs?" Babe asked.

"Probably," I said.

"You think they love the baby?"

"I guess." I jumped off beside her, remembering the pressure of her kiss. "Love's a good thing, if you can keep it."

"Race you back," she challenged.

When we got back the doctor was leaving and Sib was getting into the truck. "Where've you two been? It's time to go home." We all four squeezed into the front seat. Babe sat on Daddy Bert's lap, I sat in the middle, and Sib drove. All the stars were out.

Sib said, "We'll have to go tomorrow and pick out another tree. Will, you and Babe up for that?"

We said we were.

Daddy Bert pointed to the constellations and gave them silly names, like Babe's Hair Band and Will's Baseball Glove. We pretended we saw them in the sky.

I felt glad to be part of this family. I would feel part of it again tomorrow. And when I saw my father on Christmas Day, I would tell him about everything. He might notice how much I had grown.

Sib let me drive the truck the last mile and a half home.

Washed

Until recently Ariel Dawson thought that love was a lie.

For years her mother told her that people could fool themselves into loving someone before they realized that nothing about love was true. "You'll see," her mother said. "There are so many ways you can be fooled." The warning lodged in Ariel's mind like a mantra, and at age twenty-seven she struggled not to believe her mother's words. Then one morning Ariel found three big words in blue chalk written on the sidewalk outside her house: SOMEBODY LOVES YOU. Capitalized.

She saw the words first from the kitchen window, then went outside to look at them closely. The words faced the house, so she felt they were meant for her personally. She looked to see if the author had left a name.

Ariel had two men in her life, but one was Bernie Hockaday, who was not imaginative or romantic. She had been seeing him for almost a year, and had never been tempted to do more than kiss him. Sam Healey was a different story.

Sam arrived in town at the end of summer, tall in his army uniform. When he saw Ariel in The Frog Leg Grill, he sat down beside her in a booth. He didn't know that she was manager and part owner of The Grill, but when he learned, he teased her about being rich and famous. Both were surprised at the immediacy of their affections.

Ariel picked up her newspaper on the sidewalk. She wondered if the paperboy had seen the words in blue chalk, or what her neighbors would think as they went to work.

As she went back into the house, sunlight quivered on the air. A light breeze touched her face and made her feel kissed. She noticed that the yard needed cutting, and even that aspect of her life seemed exciting now. She imagined calling her mother about the sidewalk message. She wanted to prove her mother wrong about love.

She washed the few dishes she had used and placed them in the drainer. As she dressed for work, she could not stop going to the window. From upstairs she saw even more clearly the sidewalk message shining toward the house. Ariel tried to picture someone actually writing the words. She thought of the emotion behind the act. The words seemed part of her yard, her house, and she felt the personal import of the message—its placement and capitalization.

Janice, one of the new waitresses at The Grill, called and told Ariel that one of the refrigerators had broken down, that food needed to be moved and the rear freezer wasn't big enough. What should they do?

"Cook it," Ariel told her. "We'll have a special on burgers—
two for the price of one. We'll charge a little more for the
cobblers and pies." Ariel had been running The Frog Leg Grill
for three years, and it was now the most popular café in Lundy,
Virginia.

She slipped on her shoes, locked the house, and drove to
work, speeding most of the way; but she couldn't forget the
image, the scrawly shape of the words on the sidewalk. The
memory of those words made her day seem slow and unhurried.

All morning she waited for Sam to come into The Grill. He had
taken a job as a car mechanic and he almost always came in for
supper at six o'clock. Ariel liked to sit with him in his booth. She
would read articles from the *National Enquirer* or the *Star* to make
him laugh. At five-thirty she saw him cross the street. She
watched until he went by the place where the *G* in "Grill" and
the *og* in "Frog" were burned out. She waved him inside.

"Meat loaf sandwich and fries," he yelled to Janice, while
Ariel sat across from him in the booth and took out a copy of the
Star.

"Iowa Woman Sells Arm for Photo of Elvis." She read the
headline and showed him the front page, which featured a picture of a middle-aged woman who had lost her arm. The woman
held up a photograph of Elvis, and her left arm was cut off to a
stub at the elbow. Her name was Phyllis Goode, and she was
smiling.

"They don't convince *me* with that arm," Sam said. He
pointed to the picture. "I mean, look."

The photographer had figured a way to smudge away the

arm, but in the process had erased part of the woman's dress and waistline. The article described Phyllis Goode's obsession with Elvis, and claimed that Elvis had visited with her several times since his death. Mrs. Goode had been married for twenty years but wasn't now. She had two grown children.

Ariel watched Sam Healey's mouth as he talked about Mrs. Goode. His mouth was small and tight, and she imagined kissing it, making it full with her own kissing. And even though she made fun of people like Phyllis Goode, she understood the woman's strong feelings for Elvis. Then Ariel pretended to read another headline: "Man Writes Words of Love"—she paused— "on Woman's Sidewalk."

"You have any banana pudding left over from yesterday?" Sam asked.

"Some," she said, and closed the paper. She called for Janice to bring Sam the rest of the banana pudding. Janice put it down in front of him, and Ariel said, "On the house." She gave what she thought was a bold smile. Sam looked at her without blinking.

At night when Ariel thought about Sam Healey, she felt washed, like a wall with water running down it. Maybe not a wall meant to be washed, but washed all the same. She felt scrubbed clean by the blue chalk words that, even after several days, were still there when she got home. She hoped it wouldn't rain. She hoped the words could survive a rain.

The next evening Sam asked if she'd like to go somewhere Friday night. He had walked her home once from The Grill, but had never before suggested they go out.

"Sure." Ariel tried to act calm. The truth was she had already made plans with Bernie for Friday night but decided at that moment to break them.

She suspected she kept seeing Bernie because her father had said he was a "good man," and because he had been a comfort to her when her father died. Her father had been a minister at the First Baptist Church in Lundy, and Bernie was a faithful member.

Bernie had invited her to go with him to the Shriners' Ball on Friday. He was not a Shriner but hoped one day to be one.

"I can't go with you on Friday night, Bernie," she told him.

"But I already have the tickets," Bernie said. He pointed to his pants pocket, and Ariel wondered if he carried the tickets around with him.

"I'm sorry, Bernie. I have something I have to do. I'm sorry."

Bernie didn't answer. "Who wrote that stuff on your sidewalk?" he asked, irritated.

She stood up. "Oh, some kid," she said, turning. "Probably."

He told her to sit back down. He took her hand. "I don't know who I'm gonna get to go with me now." He wanted her to change her mind out of pity.

"Oh, Bernie," she said and touched the strings of his hair. "You'll find somebody."

After her father's death, Ariel's mother moved to Raleigh, North Carolina, and though Raleigh was only a three-hour drive from Lundy, the idea that a state line lay between them made Ariel feel that her mother was very far away. Mrs. Dawson wanted to be far from sad memories, but she did not want to sell the house. She asked Ariel to live there, and she called several times a week with instructions and warnings.

"Don't forget to lock the doors. If you don't lock up, somebody could come in and take everything you own. And I'm not even saying what they might do to you."

"Nobody's going to break in."

"Anybody could."

"I locked up," said Ariel. She wanted to get off the phone. She was tired of hearing so many warnings about life. Ariel had always wished for a mother who wouldn't warn her about everything, who instead might mention possibilities, or hope. But those warnings had begun early, when Ariel was fourteen and boys had begun to arrive at her door.

"Oh, sweetheart," her mother said, "you mustn't put too much store in boys."

"But they like me."

"You can't trust that kind of liking."

"What do you mean?" Ariel asked.

"I mean, dear, that they will tell you anything. They pretend to like you to get what they want."

"No they don't."

"You mustn't believe them. You'll be made a fool of, or worse."

"Worse than what?"

"They can take away your whole life," her mother said.

But Ariel watched boys hang around the corners of the school building—their nervous legs and fidgety hands. She wanted them to speak to her as she walked by. She wanted them to touch her thighs and face. To cup their hands on her tiny breasts. She thought of the power they had to say things they didn't mean, and to take away somebody's whole life.

On Friday night Sam arrived at Ariel's house in his rusty truck. She saw him step around the sidewalk message. He stopped to read it, then laughed and looked at Ariel in the upstairs window.

"I'll be down in a minute," she called. "Come on in."

She had a new, low-cut khaki blouse. Most of her clothes were khaki-colored. She thought the color made her eyes appear gray, though no one had actually told her it was so. She put on the blouse and a red skirt. Her hair was short now, shorter than when her father was alive. She carefully drew on lipstick the color of her skirt and rubbed rouge onto her cheeks. Her eyes looked large, and her mouth became prominent with short hair. Ariel tucked her blouse tighter into her skirt so the neckline would show the whole expanse of her shoulders and the tops of her breasts. She was glad her mother was not downstairs.

October was still warm in Lundy. Leaves were beginning to turn, and maple trees bloomed into hot red and orange. She heard Sam downstairs. He turned on the radio in the kitchen.

"There," Ariel said, speaking into the mirror. She often spoke out loud to herself, and there were times while driving when she said funny things, said them out loud and made herself laugh. She wondered if she had created another person within to keep herself company.

She heard "Autumn Leaves" playing, as it did every autumn. The music wafted into the hallway and up the stairs, and she felt like someone in a movie. She knew that a significant change was happening inside her and hoped she wasn't getting the flu.

They went to dinner at a place outside town. On the way home Sam put his arm around her. The odor of his skin was musty, like mushrooms, and Ariel kept thinking *Jesus, Jesus,* but she didn't say this out loud. That night, in bed, she cupped her hands to breathe in his smell. She fell asleep with her hands near her face.

Even after nine days, Ariel could still see the blue message from her upstairs window. Each morning, as she left, she stepped over the words, then looked for them again when she came home at night. She was glad Sam never mentioned writing them. Such silent declaration seemed irrefutable. For the first time in her life, Ariel felt loved.

When she was away from the house she liked to picture the configuration of words, and as she did she believed that love might not be a lie after all. But on the twelfth day, while she was at work, a heavy rain washed the words away. She could make out only hints of the letters.

Ariel hated knowing that the words would not be there when she woke the next morning. She considered writing them again herself. She had loved seeing them first thing, then leaving the house knowing they would be there when she got back, like a beloved pet. And though Ariel had not been drunk in several years, as she took a few cautious sips of rum she remembered what it felt like. She felt drunk thinking about it.

When Sam called and suggested a picnic on Saturday, she was already feeling mellow.

"What's wrong?" he said. "You sound funny."

"The rain washed off all of the blue chalk message," she told him.

"Oh," he said. "I was beginning to get jealous of that message anyway." He wanted her to know what he felt. "I mean, you were liking the sidewalk more than *me*."

"I'm going to bed now," she told him and hung up. She didn't want him to say more. She hoped he would write the words again before morning.

Sam picked her up before noon on Saturday, and they drove in near silence to the river. They ate from a picnic basket under a tree, and finally Ariel asked him why he was so quiet.

"I have to leave soon," he said. "For the Middle East." But he didn't say when they were sending him, and he didn't want to talk about it. He wanted to go to his parents' house and tell them, so he asked Ariel to go with him.

"It'll take about four hours to get there," he said, and suggested they spend the night. He told Ariel she would like seeing their farmhouse. They had a cat, he said. He knew she loved cats.

Ariel agreed to go but couldn't stop thinking about the fact of his leaving. Everything that had seemed right seemed suddenly wrong, and she began to take leave of him in her mind. Her mother's warnings swarmed through her head. Even her body grew stiff, creating a hard line against departure. As she agreed to go with him, she imagined she was telling him goodbye.

"I'm going away," he said, "but I'm not going away from you."

She thought he could read her mind.

Sam bit his lip. The mood between them was changing, so he suggested they swim in the river. Sam began to remove his shoes and socks. Ariel slipped off her own shoes quickly, standing barefoot; then she pulled her shirt over her head. She was not wearing a bra.

"Whoa!" he said, without meaning for her to stop.

"So what do you think?" she asked.

Sam made a sound in his throat and took off his pants. Mosquitoes began to congregate on his arms and back. Ariel pulled off her jeans and underpants. She ran toward the river, her buttocks white and shaky.

Sam ran after her. The sun had not gone all the way down, but the moon was coming up huge and orange. She told him to hurry and he yelled something, something silly, as they raced toward the water.

Ariel had already jumped in and stood in water up to her waist. "Come on," she teased as though they had known each other for a long time, as though they were not saying good-bye.

Sam stepped into the water. He was still in his underwear but pulled them off. "What do you think would happen if a snake came up right now?" he said.

"Don't," she said. "Why are you always teasing?"

"I'm not. I don't think I'm ever really teasing, but I make it sound like I am—just in case."

"I guess you think you can scare me." Ariel slipped her breasts beneath the water to make him come in.

"I *did* scare you," he yelled and jumped in. "For a minute I did." His voice was gravelly with desire. He seemed so young at that moment, she didn't know how he would behave in a war.

She swam away from him, then swam back and let him touch her in the water. His hands moved slippery along her smooth body.

"Do you love me?" she asked. She wanted to sound firm. "Because if you don't, I don't want to."

He held her waist and let his hands move around her rib cage. "I don't know," he said, but without conviction. His hands continued to explore her back and arms. "I think so. I think I do." He waited, his expression tentative, full of desire.

They held each other for a long moment before Ariel sighed. "Oh, okay." She relaxed into his arms. "You'll be leaving soon anyhow," she said, in way of explanation. She could feel the sticky mud beneath their feet.

Ariel loved to be touched. Sam said he had never seen a woman who loved so much to be touched. Not once did she tell him to stop, though at one point she cried out because she thought they had stepped on something live.

Sam made love to her in the water, then again in the cab of the truck. When they were through, Ariel said how she hoped she wouldn't die young. She said she hoped they would both live to be very old. Then she said that loving somebody, really loving with all your heart, was like dying.

"Maybe we can die together," he said. His teasing always seemed on the verge of great seriousness.

"When do you leave?" she asked him. "I mean, can you tell me?"

"Right after Thanksgiving," he said, without naming a day.

On the day they left to see Sam's parents, Ariel wore a yellow dress and had her hair cut. Sam did not wear his uniform, but instead wore dark pants and a blue oxford-cloth shirt.

"Do they know you're leaving?" Ariel imagined he might not have told them.

"Yes."

It was after five o'clock when they arrived. Sam's mother came out to greet them when their car drove into the driveway. Her name was Mary and her hair was blue with tint and stiff with spray. Mr. Healey wore a new shirt. They were dressed, all of them, for a special event, but Mr. Healey was blind, and Ariel wondered why Sam hadn't mentioned it. She could not stop watching him grope for objects. When they entered the living room, a cat named Pharaoh jumped into Ariel's lap. She stroked it.

The cat had fleas so profusely that Ariel could see them come to the edge of its fur and go back in. Mrs. Healey commented, with some embarrassment, on the fleas and said she had meant to put some flea powder on Pharaoh before they came.

"I'll do it," said Ariel. She couldn't stand to see the cat scratching constantly.

Mrs. Healey watched Ariel apply the powder from front to back. "I'd been planning to do that," she said.

They ate a dinner of meatloaf made with onion soup, cheese, and sour cream—a favorite of Sam and Mr. Healey's. Ariel ate as much as she could. They also ate a bing cherry salad, and a blackberry cobbler that was the best Ariel had ever tasted. She asked for the recipe.

"I can't stand to think of Sam going over there," said Mrs. Healey. She wanted to be reassured.

"Don't, Mary." Mr. Healey groped for the basket of rolls. "Don't make him talk about it before he even finishes his supper."

Later that evening the cat got sick—grew lethargic and vomited blood. No one mentioned that this might have been a reaction to the powder, even though Ariel kept saying, "Do you think it was the flea powder?"

"I hope this doesn't mean something bad," said Mrs. Healey. She grew visibly upset, but no one comforted her. "I hope it isn't some kind of sign."

Pharaoh shed tufts of hair from his hind end and finally Sam suggested they take it to the vet. They did not get home until ten o'clock. Mrs. Healey led Ariel to the large guest room with high ceilings and a four-poster bed. Mr. Healey followed them, then turned to say good night. He smiled a stupid, benign smile but thought no one noticed him.

Ariel put the stopper into the deep claw-foot tub, filled it with steamy water, and climbed in. She could hear Sam moving around in the next room. He came in without knocking. Ariel laid a washrag across her breasts. "Was that your room when you were little?"

"Umm-hmm." He knelt beside the tub and lifted the wet washrag.

"What're you doing?"

"Nothing. I just wanted to see you."

She smiled. "You *have* seen me." She covered herself with her hands. "What if your parents hear us?"

"They've gone to bed."

She took the washrag and soaped it, rubbing her arms.

"Let me do that." He knew how to touch her. Sam was not afraid of loving somebody.

"Sam?"

"Hmm?" He washed her arms and back with long strokes. Ariel poked her fingers through the curls of his hair, and could barely take her eyes from his face. She leaned back and let him bathe her.

"Why didn't you tell me your father was blind?" Her eyes stayed closed and she couldn't help but wonder what else he hadn't told her.

"I didn't know what you'd think. You might not've come here, or else you would've been nervous."

"I was nervous anyway," she said.

"More nervous, I mean." He moved his hands to her breasts and drew small circles.

She had never asked him directly about the words on the sidewalk. To keep the message a secret felt romantic. Besides, she did not want to know if someone else had written the words. She didn't want to ask.

He stopped his motions, then pulled off his own clothes and got into the water beside her. "I want to think of you when I'm gone," he told her.

Ariel laid back her head. She felt the old film of distrust

settle over her like dust. She wanted to throw off the film. She wanted to believe Sam would think about her.

"Will you think of me?" He wanted to force an answer. "I mean, will you write me and stuff?"

"I'll write to you," she said, as though she had made a decision larger than the question.

Sam's strong body lay beside her in the tub. She grew enchanted with his hips and legs, the extreme whiteness of his belly. She thought of the way he walked when he came to see her, and his face when he leaned over the booth at The Grill to kiss her. In the last few weeks he had let everyone see him kiss her. Now his face bloomed with light when she said, "I'll write to you. I'll even send you packages."

That was when he told her he would leave the next Saturday.

The nightly news kept track of the Gulf War's progression. Ariel wrote letters and sent packages, but she could not join the country's patriotic fervor. She heard from Sam every week for a while, then the letters did not come so often.

"Have you heard from Sam?" her mother asked. "I've been watching the war on TV."

"I've gotten some letters."

"Well, just don't put all your eggs in one basket."

"Why do you say that? Why do you always say something like that?" Ariel could feel tears well up into her throat and voice.

"I don't want you to get hurt," she said. "That's all. I don't want you to look like a fool."

The fact was that Ariel had not heard from Sam in a month.

What made her keep faith was the fact that two nights before Sam was scheduled to fly to Iraq, she awoke one morning to see again the words scrawled on the sidewalk: SOMEBODY LOVES YOU.

She imagined Sam sneaking back to town to write it. She admired how he could not hide his affection, how it came out in ways that were so visible and public. She wished to touch him, to smell the back of his neck. She sat beside her window for a long time, reading the bold words over and over.

That night she had crawled into bed and dreamed of being a person with an enormous appetite sitting at an empty table, but the table kept changing before her eyes, becoming a complete banquet, a feast. She woke up feeling as though she had already eaten.

After the New Year, when she had heard from Sam only three times, and after Valentine's Day had come and gone, Mr. Healey called Ariel to say that Sam was coming home on March 12, and that he wanted Ariel to meet him at their house. Could she do it? Mary Healey was on the other line and said she hoped Ariel could find her way. They would mail directions to her. They told her they had not been receiving Sam's letters either, but that Sam would call her in the next week.

"How is Pharaoh?" Ariel asked.

"He's just fine," said Mr. Healey. "It seems he was allergic to flea powder but not to fleas." She could hear him chuckle. Even on the phone, he sounded blind.

That night a storm was predicted. Ariel loved storms. Even as a child, whenever storms came, her life seemed on a specific course. Rain, hard rain, made her feel courageous.

Finally, she called her mother to say that Sam was returning in March.

"He is?"

"Yes. And yesterday I got a packet of letters. He'd been writing to me the whole time, but they all came at once. And he wants me to meet him at his parents' house." She felt her words held an air of importance. She wanted to say, "See, see?"

"Don't expect too much," her mother said, but Ariel was expecting everything.

When she drove up to the house, Mr. Healey stood in the yard with a dog that had been purchased since her last visit. Pharaoh slept in the window. As her car entered the driveway, the dog stood up and Mr. Healey lifted his head toward the car's sound.

Sam came out and ran to greet Ariel. He lifted her out of the car and swung her around. Mary Healey stood on the porch with her hands on her mouth. She ushered them into the house, where she had a platter of ham biscuits and a stack of pancakes with melted butter and dark syrup. She motioned for everyone to sit down. Sam passed around some photos of places he had been. The people who stood before the camera looked desolate. Some were not Americans.

"Did you spend all your time in Riyadh, son?" Mr. Healey asked. "Was there much danger?"

"I'm not supposed to talk about it." Sam put away the pictures and reached for more pancakes. "They told me not to talk about my experiences over there." His expression looked sheepish.

"You're not?" Ariel could not take her eyes off him. Sam

seemed suddenly important because he had a secret he was not supposed to speak about. And that secret belonged to the nation, and had to do with war. He looked handsome sitting there, heroic.

"Yeah." Sam put empty dishes into the sink by leaning back in the chair and sliding them in. "I probably shouldn't have shown you the photos. I don't know why I said anything."

"Just lonesome, I guess." Mary Healey liked to give simple answers to hard questions. She made excuses for people in tight spots; but she seemed relieved, because until that moment the war had not seemed real to her.

"I didn't tell you about the sparrow yet," Ariel said, and she told Sam how a bird had flown into the half-opened window of her car one night when she was driving home from work, and had died in the seat beside her. She was approaching a stop sign when she saw it. Then she heard, more than saw, the bird enter through a small space above the window's ledge. His neck lay curved and his head limp. "I thought its neck was broken. I stopped the car and watched it die." The bird was small, a sparrow, she thought.

"I pulled off the road and lifted it out, and I had the funniest feeling that it might come alive in my hands." She laid it at the base of a big willow tree, and dug a small hole with a stick. "When I lifted it again," she said, "its wings started to flutter, and its eyes opened, fast. I couldn't believe it." As Ariel watched it regain a natural grace and fly off, she felt as if she had been given something wild—a whole new life. "I could not believe it." She laughed out loud.

"That doesn't even sound true," Sam said.

Ariel felt hurt. "A lot of things that don't sound true are," she told him.

"We've been watching the war on TV," his mother said. She got up to start the dishes.

"We'll do the dishes," Ariel offered. "We'll clean up."

Ariel began to clear away the plates and piled them into the sink. Sam's father left for a walk and his mother said she believed she would take a nap.

"Wanna help me, Healey?" Ariel spoke the name she would call Sam for the next forty-five years.

"Okay."

They stood at the sink, looking out the window at Sam's blind father led by a dog along the ridge of a levee. Ariel could not say what happened at that moment, or why she found herself believing in the same things she believed in when it rained. The wall of her body had been washed. She felt like one of those products that until water is added does not become what it really is. Then in a quiet voice, she told Sam that she loved him.

Sam knew the difficulty of those words for Ariel. He stood behind her and put his arms around her arms in the water. He let drops of dishwater fall onto one of her breasts. She turned around to rub suds on his face, making a mustache and beard, then she rubbed them off with her thumbs.

"You remember when you wrote those words on my sidewalk?" she asked. "When you wrote 'Somebody Loves You' in big blue letters?" Ariel lifted herself to sit on the edge of the sink. She laughed to let him know she knew he had done it.

"I didn't write that." Sam looked past her out the window. "I saw it, but I didn't write it."

"You didn't?"

"No."

Her face felt drained of blood, her expectations broken. "But it was there again, just before you left. I was so sure you'd done it."

Sam didn't answer. He didn't say how love could begin, or even flourish, under a false presumption—the same as war.

"Oh well," he said. "I *should* have written it." He smiled, his face full of promise. "You want me to *say* I wrote it?"

"No."

All this time Ariel had imagined something that wasn't true, and now it didn't matter. The door was already open.

What was true was stronger than what had been in her imagination. If she asked him to, he would write those words. But she knew, too, that *she* might scrawl those same words for him on any sidewalk, or wall.

That's what she had been waiting for: to do the loving part herself. She could feel her heart inside her own chest, like a light in a closet. The door had been opened and she wanted to tell her scared mother, her dead father, or anybody who might listen— Somebody Loves You. She wanted them to believe it.

Sam moved his hand onto her back and pulled her toward him. Ariel sat precariously on the edge of the sink, wrapping her long legs around his waist.

"I think I might be dying," she said, her voice dramatic, hopeful.

"Who isn't?" he told her and lifted her from the sink, swinging her around in circles. Her legs stayed tight around his waist, her hands like birds on his shoulders. Then she let her head fall back as he swung her around. They moved over the floor, turning, balanced as dancers.

A Sounding Brass

It was one of those hot Augusts in southern Georgia when the days are especially long and nights rise up softly out of the ground almost without any notice, until suddenly it is late, ten o'clock, and the children are still outside. But they had not noticed the dark had come, had settled onto the objects around them. Ginny, too, was surprised at how the night had crept up.

"Come on in," she called to her children, and they ran across the yard. They raced to the refrigerator, and Jay grabbed his sister's shirt to hold her back, then touched the refrigerator door twice, letting her know that he had won. Nell began a long plea as Jay looked to his mother, trying to judge if he would be reprimanded.

Nell was nine and always on the verge of tears. Ginny put her hand on the little girl's back and told her to take a bath, that the tub was already full. Nell jerked away and looked at her mother with the expression of someone who has been asked to sell everything.

Jay was twelve. He walked with a swagger identical to his father's. Ginny knew he felt the need to take his father's place in the household, and that he had felt that burden since William's death. She tried to relieve him of it.

"What's the matter?" he asked his mother, deciding to take the reprimand. He had made a sandwich of turkey and ham and cheese, with mustard spilling out the sides. He licked his fingers.

Ginny thought about the resilience of children, their natural ability for self-preservation, and how at a certain age that ability seemed to be forgotten or overrun by other things. And you begin to wonder if those things will end, or if they will end you.

"What's the matter?" He wanted to get it over with.

"Nothing," said Ginny. She could see mustard at the corners of his mouth.

In the last few months Jay had grown taller than his mother, and he liked to kiss the top of her head to demonstrate his height. He leaned now to kiss where her hair parted in the middle. Ginny wiped mustard from his mouth with her thumb, two quick, efficient swipes, the way she had done when he was three. She felt sure she had some in her hair. Jay sat down at the table.

"Lemuel called," Ginny said. Jay turned to her, not knowing what to ask.

"What'd he say?"

"He wants to come here for a visit." Ginny brought a glass of milk and set it on the table. "On Saturday." It seemed a question.

"I'd like to see him," said Jay.

Neither spoke for a moment, and Ginny pictured Lemuel as he stood at the back door that morning, with the paper and his odd, dry look.

Ginny, William, and the children had left home for a vacation trip in March. They were to spend two weeks in a rented house on the Carolina coast. The house was spacious, with a huge porch built on stilts, and each year for the past seven years they had rented the same place from a man named Lemuel Watkins. The house, on a strip of private beach, faced the sea. No trees grew in the yard, but scraggly bushes poked out of the sand, going to the limit of their growth.

William had driven all night in a hurry to begin the vacation, not able to consider it begun until they reached their destination. When they arrived, the children preferred the crowds farther down the beach and went looking for new and old friends. But Ginny loved their privacy. She loved midnight swims that ended on the sand, then in the outside shower, and on the bedroom floor. As she looked back on that time, she felt glad to have had those days with William as their last.

Each morning at the beach Ginny rose earlier than the others. She liked to fix breakfast without the need for hurry and organization that her regular mornings demanded. She spooned coffee into the heavy black percolator that came with the house, and placed it squarely on the eye of the stove.

She heard four quick shots from the woods across the street, and from the kitchen window could see two young boys with guns. She wanted to call out to them "Be careful" or something admonishing, but decided not to. She slipped off her shoes to walk on the beach for a half hour, and returned to the house with its fresh-perked coffee smell.

William would usually be sitting at the table when she finished her walk; but this morning she stood at the stove and wondered how late he would sleep. A low knock at the door alarmed her. As she turned around, Lemuel Watkins mumbled something and handed her the morning paper. William and Ginny knew Mr. Watkins, but the kids knew him better and called him by his first name. They visited his house every year. Lemuel had two grandsons who were always glad to see Jay and Nell.

Ginny reached for the paper and welcomed him in. "William's not up yet," she said, and offered him some coffee. He waved his hand to indicate that he didn't want coffee and pointed in the direction of the sun.

Ginny could not tell how old he was, but suspected he was not as old as he looked. His hair was white-gray and his face, though lined, was not wrinkled. He had a dryness about him. His skin and hair and voice were raspy. She thanked him for the paper, but as he did not turn to leave, she thanked him again with a finality that sounded slightly rude, then motioned for him to sit down. He sat in the biggest, most comfortable chair. Ginny stood at the kitchen counter.

In the distance they could hear sirens, and Ginny felt apprehensive, deciding her nervousness had to do with Lemuel's sudden intrusion. When she sat down, he leaned toward her. "It's about William," he said in a grave voice.

William had heard shots from the woods across the street and had not been able to return to sleep. Ginny was out walking. He dressed and went to the woods, seeing two boys about Jay's age, maybe younger. They were shooting at wood larks and squirrels, not hitting much of anything but not caring either. He warned them about pointing the guns toward the house, then asked where they were staying. They said, "With our granddaddy, Lemuel." William laughed and said he hadn't recognized them.

"One of the boys stepped forward," Lemuel said, "but he tripped on a root and the gun threw itself up." He shifted, and touched Ginny's arm. "The gun hit against William's chest. The boy tried to catch it, but when he did, he pulled the trigger." Ginny sat on the floor, her legs giving way. "The gun fired." Lemuel took hold of her arm.

"Where is he? Is he okay?"

"I called the hospital and the police. I came over here and looked in. I didn't see anybody around."

"The children are asleep," Ginny said. She had not moved to get up. "Do they know?"

"I wanted to find you first," said Lemuel. He offered his hand. "He was alive for a little while."

Ginny stood, moving like someone drunk. Lemuel led her to the place in the woods where William's long body crumpled over his legs. One arm hung outward as if he were reaching. For the gun, probably, Ginny thought.

"He's all right," she said out loud, then reached down to move his arms into a more comfortable position. She looked around wondering where the two boys were.

"They're at home," Lemuel said, guessing her thoughts.

Ginny did not want to look again at William lying there. She turned toward the horizon. She was glad Lemuel was with her, but part of her blamed him. Not for the death exactly, but for bringing the news and for his connection to the event. As she spoke, she began to yell accusations about him, about his grandsons. She wanted for someone to be responsible. Lemuel accepted the storm, but his body started with indignation, quiet in his defense.

When Ginny was through (her arms wildly gesturing, her eyes drained of all their resistance), she turned to see a crowd of people and ambulances; but for months she kept in her mind the image of the old man at the screen door handing her the paper, the news.

She walked away from the woods and toward the house where her children still slept. She woke them, told them to dress quickly, then they followed the ambulance to the hospital.

"Is he dead?" asked Nell. "What happened? I don't get it." She spoke as if this were a trick.

"Yes." Ginny could not look at their faces. They both sat next to her in the front seat.

"I want to see him," said Jay.

So they spent the day at the hospital deciding how to send William's body home. The next day Lemuel helped them pack the car. They arrived home five days after they had started their vacation, and on the seventh day they buried William.

Ginny thought of how she had gotten into bed that night after the service, slipping between the cold sheets as if she had to be careful not to spill anything. She felt that if one drop spilled, one drop of what she felt, everything would pour out. So she lay flat in the vacancy of her room, sightless and inconsolable. When her grief came, it came as the sound of a cello, or a bassoon.

• • •

When Ginny had gone upstairs, Nell took her bath and now sat in the middle of her bed eating potato chips. She wore pajama bottoms, and a towel piled high on her head. Each night she surrounded herself with objects, arranging them in a certain way on her bed so that she could count or touch them before sleeping. She rubbed the smooth stomach of a silver and bronze fish bought by her father a few years ago. The head of the fish was silver, and the body bronze, with gills carved in delicate streaks along the sides. The fish had its mouth open, and its strange lips curled as if it were about to drink. Nell liked to wear the fish around her neck, to rub its icy, polished head. She liked to put her finger over its mouth, or to lift the mouth to her eye, then to Ginny's eye—its small hollow body so dark they could not see anything.

Ginny lifted the towel, and Nell's hair fell wet and stringy to her shoulders. They combed out the knots and Nell pulled the covers over her legs, leaving her chest exposed. Her tiny-nippled breasts had barely begun to swell. Ginny pulled a package of cookies from her pocket. Nell unwrapped them, ate two, then put the wrapper in a drawer filled with other bits of paper and wrappers she could not throw away.

"It wasn't fair," Nell said, almost whispering.

"What wasn't?"

"That Jay pulled my shirt and kept me from winning. I would've won."

"I know," Ginny said, and the recognition and agreement seemed to be enough.

"Lemuel's coming on Saturday," Ginny finally told her.

Nell seemed glad, but reserved her gladness until she saw what her mother wanted.

"It'll be good to see him, don't you think?" Ginny picked things off the bed and placed them on Nell's shelf.

"Yeah." Nell motioned with her hands. "Not there. Don't put that there. I always put that on the table and the fish on the bottom shelf by the harmonica."

"Oh." Ginny wondered what peculiar order Nell saw for this shelf.

"And books go at the top," she added. Then she spoke suddenly, feeling permission for enthusiasm. "When will he get here?"

"We'll pick him up at the train on Saturday."

They had seen Lemuel in May. He had kept in touch with them, writing letters, sometimes calling. Ginny explained that he felt guilty and probably needed to stay in touch with them. Nell had told him one night on the phone that maybe they would come back to the beach to see him. Ginny was shocked to hear her suggestion.

"Why did you say that?" Ginny asked. "We're not going back."

Nell cried and Jay explained to his mother that Nell "pretended that Dad was still there and if they went back she might find him." Ginny had to admit that part of her felt the same way. No one knew what Jay thought.

Jay was already in bed by the time she had tucked in Nell. He would not call his mother to tell him good night anymore. The nightly ritual of being tucked into bed was too juvenile for him now. But he seemed pleased when his mother knocked at the door asking permission to come in. She told him good night in an offhand way, and kissed him while straightening the covers. When she turned out the light, he spoke to her through the dark. "Anytime," he said.

A summer rain drummed suddenly against the roof and trees. Ginny could hear thunder, but the pounding felt as if it went on inside her, a strong, washing rhythm. As she listened, her skin came alive, the blood pulsing away the seconds—not as if she were losing them, just feeling them move through her. Then, at the height of the moment, when everything around her was attuned to the pounding rhythm of the rain, she became alarmed at how alone she was.

She undressed and felt cold, not wanting the warmth of her robe, or the blanket at the foot of the bed, but needing another warmth. She slipped her nightgown over her head and looked at herself in the mirror. She wondered how she looked to men.

A month ago she had attended a party, where her friends encouraged her to enjoy male companionship. She found she did not know how to be with men anymore.

As Ginny thought of William, she felt chilled to the bone and sat down. She rubbed her arms, an instinct, a response that gave her the warmth she needed. And she wondered if other people did this—rubbed their arms at the right time and found comfort.

Lemuel arrived at the house at three o'clock. They were surprised, since they had planned to pick him up at the train.

"I got here earlier than I thought," he said. Nell took his hand

and led him to her room. Jay followed, talking to Lemuel's back. Lemuel nodded. They liked having him, for the first time, on their own turf.

"Let Lemuel sit down," said Ginny.

Lemuel's face had grown thin and his arms hung long. He had the appearance of bending. Nell showed him the tiny silver and bronze fish, letting him look into its mouth and turn it with his hands. Jay boasted about baseball and showed Lemuel his trophies. Lemuel, for the moment, looked like part of the family, and though Ginny attributed the closeness to their sharing of an irrevocable event, still, when she thought of it, she was amazed.

Jay asked Lemuel to come with him into the backyard. He wanted to show him a tree whose trunk rose up straight, then veered sharply horizontal before rising again. "It looks like somebody tried to knock it down," said Jay.

"And failed," said Lemuel. The tree had absorbed the blow. A knob formed at the place where the trunk curved up again, and the curve had a look of force, as if great strength had been focused on that one place.

Bark covered the lower half, so that when you stood close to the tree, it looked similar to other trees, but when you looked up, you could see where the bark had stopped growing, and underneath a white wood shone. As the tree got higher, it grew thinner and whiter, like a bone; and the leaves that grew grew high at the top, where the pith flowered into branches. Jay asked Lemuel what made the knobby part turn like that, and Lemuel said that something had happened to it when it was young. Jay asked if that could happen again, farther up, and Lemuel said no.

"The children seem all right," Lemuel told Ginny as he sat at the kitchen table, their first moments alone.

Ginny placed dishes into the cupboard. "Yes," she said. "I think so."

"And how about you?" Lemuel took a dish from her hand and led her to the table.

"I'm okay." Her voice sounded brittle. "Or will be." She sat down quickly, then he sat, but a moment passed before he spoke.

"When I was a boy," he began, "and lived in Kentucky, I met an immigrant family."

His words startled Ginny into a focused attention.

"They were from Poland. They came to town in the spring and set up house on a hill near the railroad tracks. The man was hardworking. He found a job at the mill. His wife took in ironing for a few families, including mine." He leaned back in his chair, like a man telling a long story. "So I'd been inside the house to pick up the starched shirts and my mother's dresses. The house always smelled like fresh-baked bread and steam."

Ginny watched him, bewildered but attentive.

"Every Saturday I walked down the railroad tracks to pick up laundry and I'd usually stop by the country store for a Grapette. Sometimes I'd stay at the store awhile, but this day I saw the Polish girl waving to me from her house, telling me to hurry. The girl was ten, two years younger than myself. I ran to see what was wrong." Now Lemuel leaned forward. He wanted to speak to Ginny in the intimate way of story.

"Her mother lay on the couch. Somebody had covered her with a stained blanket. The room didn't smell like bread anymore, and the mother's face looked dull, her eyes rolled back into her head. I thought maybe she was dead, then she spoke, but she spoke Polish. When I asked what she had said, the girl told me she was talking about a fire she'd been in years ago. The girl said her mother had been calling for people they never heard of, and that her father had gone for the doctor. He wasn't back yet and that was two hours ago."

Ginny shifted in her chair.

"A little boy, her brother I think, stood in the corner of the room. He played with a wooden truck. He was about three years old. He didn't cry but stood very still, and his hands rolled the truck along the wall. The girl said she didn't know what to do, then she said, 'She's dying, isn't she?' And I said I didn't know, but that it looked like it. I asked if her mother could recognize her.

"The girl shivered and she looked at her mother's face. It was gray. She told me to sit down. The house was poor but well-kept, and clothes were draped over the backs of chairs. All the tables were made of dark wood, except the one where they ate: a large block table that had thick legs. I'd never seen one like it and thought maybe they built it themselves. A big vase sat in the middle, a few branches of dogwood stuck in it, and I imagined the girl had put them there." Lemuel looked away from Ginny.

"I heard the Polish woman exhale once, and give a little hum. The girl jumped as if she'd heard a loud noise. The boy stopped rolling the truck and went to touch his mother's arm, but the girl pushed him back, nearly knocked him down. I caught the boy and went to get his truck.

"The boy asked me, 'Is she asleep?' I said she was. But the

girl"—Lemuel turned back to Ginny—"the girl had her ear to her mother's mouth. Listening, I thought, for another hum or message, because she didn't know what to do and neither did I. So I watched her as she listened to the open mouth and I hoped that when the woman spoke it wouldn't be with those cries she'd been making when I walked in, because the girl's ear was so close to her mother's mouth it would scare her."

Ginny nodded, and kept nodding as he continued.

"I went to stoke the ashes in the big stove and to place another piece of wood inside. Then I put water on to boil, because it always seemed a good thing to do at bad times. I'd seen older people turn to the stove and begin to boil or cook food at times of grief, because it helped to make everything more normal. And I knew that this was death, or I almost knew it. And I didn't want to keep watching the girl with her ear to her mother's mouth."

Ginny stood up, restless. She went to the other side of the room and leaned against the kitchen sink.

"When the girl heard water boiling, she came over and asked what I was doing. I said, 'What would you like?' and she said, 'Coffee,' pulling it down for me from the shelf. I'd never tasted coffee before, and probably neither had she; but at the time I figured she drank it every day, since she was from a foreign country and maybe did things differently.

"Then she turned to me and said it was my fault, that if I hadn't come in her mother wouldn't be dead. She even began to hit me with her fists, just hitting and yelling. Finally, I told her the coffee was ready and she sat down. The younger boy cried, though nobody comforted him.

"The coffee was almost too dark to drink. We were adding

sugar to it when the father came in, saying the doctor was on his way. He looked at his wife on the couch and at the children around the room. Then he gathered us together and held us to him for a long time, even me, squatting down to reach us all. He put his face against our chests, and the girl stood tall, letting it happen. So did the boy, and so did I. All of us standing taller than the father, but letting him reach around us and huddle us to his head."

Ginny looked out the window and nodded over the sink. The light was changing from afternoon to evening.

"The family moved away after that. I didn't know where. But the house on the hill stayed empty, and sometimes I went to see the block table they left there, too heavy to move."

Ginny waited to see what else he would say.

"I wanted to tell you that. I just wanted to tell you that story."

Ginny came back to the table and sat down. She was still nodding, though she had nothing to say. She called to tell the kids to come downstairs, that they were going to take Lemuel out for dinner.

At dinner she asked Lemuel to tell the story again, tell it to Jay and Nell, so he did. They listened, though their listening seemed more polite than interested. Ginny listened the second time with the same attention as the first. And she felt the confusion one feels when someone suggests that your ideas of what life should be will fail, and that you will not be happy in the ways you thought.

They took Lemuel to the train the next afternoon, saying goodbye and making promises to see each other again. On the way home, the children argued, and light fell on the street as it had years ago. As they rode along, Ginny noticed how the light changed in only a moment's time, and she turned her head to the trees.

The scene was both light and dark. The clouds hung heavy like a ceiling and gave the air an odd gray color above the trees. The road held a brightness that made her squint. When she looked up to see where the light was coming from, she saw no break in the clouds, and when she looked back at the road she thought the light must be coming from somewhere beneath it.

"Don't," Nell whined at her brother.

"Don't." He mocked her and repeated whatever he was doing, which made her scream, "Quit it! Quit!"

"Stop that, Jay," Ginny said absently.

Ginny told them to look at the road, at the way the light was falling and how it looked as if it were coming from the ground. They both leaned over the front seat, genuinely interested for a moment.

The wall of trees grew high along the road and made Ginny feel safe. She wanted to keep driving past the turn for her house, past the field two miles away. She wanted to prolong the elation that came as light rose from a place she did not expect, the road shimmering in front of her like a pond or a path she had chosen.

The scene entered her mind as if she were remembering it; and she knew that when she thought of this moment, years later, nothing would be lost. She was glad she had decided to drive home along this road. It was like entering a painting. But when she reached the road that headed to her house, she turned in, knowing that such moments could not be prolonged and that trying to prolong them often led to frustration and disappointment, so that the memory would then be tainted. She turned toward home but tucked the scene inside her, storing it low in her body where it would stay until old age.

"Mom," Jay said. "She tells on everything."

"You poke my ears. I hate that. How would you like to have your ears poked every second?"

He tickled her and she laughed.

Ginny slowed the car and threatened to put them both out on the side of the road and leave them there.

"Put *her* out," said Jay.

A voice came from the floorboard now. "Put *him*."

When Ginny pulled into the driveway, she wondered if it would rain, and what she would fix for dinner. Years ago, when the light had come like this, William had been standing at the stove, stirring and tasting with a wooden spoon when she came in. He said what a weird light it was and how he couldn't get over what it had looked like as he came home. She had answered yes, and kissed him full on the mouth.

The car doors opened and the children scrambled to the kitchen. Ginny heard "I won!" as they hit the refrigerator. When she got out, she heard them running to their rooms. They were laughing. It was so hot that the yard smelled like brass.

She decided to make corn bread. As she entered the kitchen, she thought of the Polish home and the man who reached his arms around the tall children. How they stood letting it happen, how he buried his head into their young chests, their warm, lively fragrance like that of blossoms or clover.

Saved

When Josie Wire walked down to the front of the tent at a revival meeting, her friend Alice was with her. The words of the preacher had stirred their hearts, and for weeks afterward they spoke of nothing but being missionaries in Africa. Alice would be a medical missionary, Josie a regular one. Both girls were twelve, though Josie would turn thirteen in June.

"My dad thinks we'll change our minds later on," Alice told Josie. "He says just wait till we get interested in boys."

But Alice was already interested in boys, and Josie dreamed of them at night. "I can't imagine changing our minds, can you?" said Josie. "I mean, I have seen pictures of Africa. I've wanted to go there even before I knew about God."

"I'm just saying what he told me," said Alice.

Alice's father was a neurologist who lived in a big house where Josie loved to spend the night. On Saturday mornings Alice and Josie sat at a table in the dining room with sun pouring through the long windows. A Spanish woman named Rosa served them eggs and bacon and hot cinnamon rolls. She said *Por favor?* if she didn't understand something.

Josie liked to try to talk to the Spanish woman. She liked to imitate her accent, and flounce around the kitchen copying Rosa. Rosa wore skirts that made her look like a flamenco dancer. She told Josie that she had grown up in Barcelona. Once Josie had walked into the kitchen and seen Alice's father standing next to Rosa with his hand on her shoulder. Rosa was barefoot, her head down, and she looked beautiful. Alice told Josie that Rosa kept some magic beads in a box by the sink.

"And whenever Rosa prays," said Alice, "she rolls those beads around in her hands."

After that, Josie stole one of her mother's worst necklaces, and when she prayed she held the necklace, rubbing each bead hard. Josie's family did not have servants, had never had them. Her own father taught history at a private school, and her mother, until recently, had worked as a clerk in a downtown store. Mrs. Wire had stopped working a few months before, and money was now tight.

Alice lived in a posh neighborhood, though it was situated not far from a housing project. The girls enjoyed walking into the poor section to give dollar bills to children or beggars. Their parents did not know they were doing this. Each Saturday since they had dedicated their lives, the girls gave away their weekly allowance to poor people.

"We've got to stop giving all our money away," said Alice. "We don't even have enough to go to the movies anymore."

"But I don't mind staying home, if it's for a good cause," said

Josie. She felt that her dedication was stronger than Alice's, and wanted Alice to feel the way she did. "There are so many people who need us."

"Like who?"

"Like that lady we gave money to today, and others who hang out in bars. People like that."

"We can't do anything for those people," said Alice.

"*Maybe* we can." Josie began to thumb through the phone book looking for the number of a bar called the Wagon Wheel. Each time she thought of its name, her blood grew excited. The bar was located not far from where Josie lived, so she passed it going to school, or to town. She grew silent trying to look inside, trying to see what was going on. On this Saturday night she suggested to Alice that they find the number and make a call to someone at that bar.

"What would we say?" asked Alice, putting her own finger on the words in the phone book. For the first time she looked excited about Josie's idea.

"We could just talk. Whoever answers, we'll just ask them about their life. It'll be good."

Since the idea was Josie's, she had to make the call. A man with a gruff voice answered.

"Yeah. Who is it?" The man was used to getting calls from wives checking up on a husband.

Josie couldn't speak.

"Hello?" said the voice.

"Uh, excuse me," Josie finally said. "To who am I speaking?" She tried to make her voice sound gravelly and older.

"Who the *hell* is this?" the man said.

Josie tried to hand the phone to Alice, but Alice wouldn't take it. "My name is Josie." She was almost shouting. "And I'm calling to see if you are a saved person or not."

"Is this a joke?" the man asked.

"You have to answer if you are saved." There, she said it. Josie could hear the tinkle of glasses and wild music in the background.

"No," he said. "I'm not." He expected a punch line.

"Do you *want* to be?" she asked.

"What does it mean?" the man asked prudently.

"It means *every*thing," said Josie, and smiled at Alice. It was working. She and Alice grew excited at the idea of their first prospect. "You won't have to worry about anything, like if you're going to heaven. Stuff like that."

"I'm not ready to die anyway," the man said.

"I mean when it's time, then you will go to be with the angels instead of to—*you* know."

"What do I have to do?" The man sounded mollified.

"You have to love Jesus," said Josie.

"Okay," the man said quickly.

"Really?"

"Yeah." The man hung up.

Josie dialed the number again.

"Yeah?" said the voice.

"Listen," said Josie. "That was mean. I just wanted to ask you about something and you hung up on me."

"We musta been cut off," said the man. "How *old* are you?"

"I'm fifteen," lied Josie, excited that the man who was *not* saved, and probably drunk, was asking her about herself. She did look fifteen. She had breasts and a deep curve at the waist; her hips moved out like little hills. She and Alice had both developed figures that were catching the eyes of boys, and men. Alice had even begun to go to the drugstore with Boog Barnett, who was the handsomest boy in the eighth grade. Boog said words like *piss* and *damn.* Sometimes Alice repeated the words. She let him put his arm around her waist and buy her Coke floats. Since her interest in Boog had accelerated around the same time as their being saved, they had talked almost as much about Boog as they had about being missionaries.

"I bet you're pretty," said the man. "I bet you look like some of the students I used to have in my classroom. What's your name?"

Josie told him her name, and said she had a friend named Alice. She and Alice shivered with the thrill of talking to a strange man on the phone at ten o'clock at night. They had not expected anyone to be friendly. "What's yours?"

"Samuel Beckett," said the man.

"That's nice. That's a nice name," said Josie, mouthing the name to Alice. "I think I've heard of you."

"I don't see how."

"What do you *do?*" Josie asked.

"I used to be a teacher but got fired."

Josie grew silent.

"I probably taught little girls like you. You don't sound so little, though." He spoke his words as though he were proffering a gift.

"What do I sound like?" she asked.

"Like a young woman. I'm wondering what you look like, though. What kind of hair do you have?"

"What do you mean?"

"I mean is it long or short, and what color is it? I'm just trying to picture what you look like."

"It's brown," said Josie. "It's kind of curly."

"Well," said the man. He was waiting to hear more.

"I thought we were talking about whether or not you were saved."

"I said I wasn't."

"But don't you want to be?"

"Depends."

"Depends on what?"

"On who's saying it. I have to hear something like that from somebody I can trust. I have to be sure the person's telling me the truth. Are you telling me the truth?"

"Oh, yes. My friend Alice will tell you too. She'll tell you the same thing. We work to*gether*."

"I don't care about any Alice," said Samuel Beckett. "I want to hear about *you*."

Josie tried not to look as pleased as she felt. Over the last couple of weeks, Alice had spent more and more time with boys, and Josie had been left alone in her quest to be faithful. She thought Alice was being drawn away from God, and Alice kept saying that you could like a boy and *still* like God. Josie didn't see how.

"I bet he's old," said Alice when they hung up. "I bet he's old and decrepit."

"He didn't sound it," said Josie. "He sounded real nice."

"How nice can he be, him being in a bar?" Alice folded back the bed and fluffed the pillows. Each of them had two large pillows on their bed. At Josie's home each person only had one pillow. It occurred to Josie that the reason Boog Barnett was asking Alice out was because Alice was rich. Alice said it was time for bed and they should say their prayers now.

"Do you think God likes jokes?" Josie asked.

"I don't know," said Alice. "Why?"

"Sometimes when I pray I tell him a joke. I think he likes for me to. I bet not many people do that." Alice said she was tired. But they talked for a while about what their life in the Congo would be like, until there came a long silence when Josie asked Alice a question about native rituals. Alice didn't answer.

"You asleep?" Josie asked, and the lack of an answer made her feel alone. Josie prayed silently for the man in the bar. Then she prayed to be sexy like the woman from Barcelona. She also prayed for her mother, who seemed to be crying all the time now.

Over the last year, whenever Josie came home she would find her mother in the kitchen with her head on her arms, crying. So one night, Josie asked her brother if their parents were going to get a divorce. The next day Mr. Wire reassured Josie that she need not worry about divorce.

"Did James tell you I asked about that?" said Josie.

"Yes," said Mr. Wire, "and I wanted you to know that your mother's sadness is about you. She worries about you, and the operation that's coming up."

A few years ago Josie had been diagnosed with aortal stenosis, and would need an operation on her heart. The operation was scheduled for August. The doctor had explained how the procedure would be performed, but he had waited for Josie to be older, stronger. Josie thought about what the doctor told her, but she hadn't worried until she saw her mother's sadness. Every night she prayed that her mother would stop crying.

On the next Friday night Josie and Alice called the Wagon Wheel again to see if the same man would answer. He didn't, and the harsh voice who spoke to Josie hung up on her. She called back, remembering the persistence of the disciples, and asked for Samuel Beckett. She tried to make her voice sound older by lowering it. She heard the gruff-voiced man call out the name "Sam Beckett?" and a long pause. When he returned to the phone he said, "Nobody here by that name," then, "Wait a minute. Here he is."

"Hello?"

"Samuel Beckett?"

"Yeah."

"It's Josie."

"Well, I recognize your voice. *Pretty* Josie." His voice slurred against itself. *"Pretty baby."* He sort of sang her name. "I sure think you oughta le' me see ya."

"Why?" said Josie. She didn't want Alice to know what he had said, but she had blushed and Alice was saying, "What? What did he say?"

"He wants to meet me," Josie mouthed. Alice sucked in her breath.

"I think if I meet you I'm more likely to see whether I wanna

be safed. You could tell me what's like, and maybe I'll be con-
finced."

He did not sound like someone who had ever been a teacher.
"Well," said Josie. "I wouldn't be able to come *there*. I'd get in
trouble if I did."

"We could meet in the park," he said. "Would you meet with
me in the park? You know how the benches have numbers on
them?"

"Yes."

"You could come to Bench Twenty-three."

"I would bring Alice with me," Josie said, but Alice was shaking her head no. "I mean, if I come, I would bring Alice."

"Sure," he slurred. "Alice is a *pretty* baby too." He hung up,
and Alice and Josie argued about whether or not to go to Bench
23 during the coming week.

"He didn't say *when* we should go. Does he think we're just
gonna go and wait every day?" Alice said.

"I don't know."

Alice and Josie went to Bench 23 on Monday afternoon, but
no one was there. Alice was relieved. They waited almost twenty
minutes.

"We probably ought to get home," Alice said. "My mom will
be worried."

They called the Wagon Wheel again the next weekend, but
this time on Sunday night, and Samuel Beckett answered the
phone. His voice was clear, not slurry.

"Hello?" Samuel Beckett said.

"I waited for you at the bench," said Josie. "I waited on Monday and you didn't come."

"I'm sorry about that," said Beckett. "I'm afraid I was drunk. But I'll meet you this Tuesday afternoon," he said. "That's my day off. Did you know that I got a part-time job as bartender? I think you're bringing me good luck."

"I *am?*"

"I might turn into a believer yet." She could tell by his voice that he was smiling, happy.

"Really?"

"I'm busy now and have to go, but you meet me on Tuesday at two o'clock."

"I don't get out of school till three-thirty."

"Four o'clock, then."

"Is it still Bench Twenty-three?" Josie asked.

"Yeah," Sam said.

"I'm not going with you this time," said Alice. "I have cheer-leading practice."

Another thing that was coming between Alice and Josie was the fact that Alice had been selected as next year's cheerleader. She was cheerleader, plus she had Boog Barnett. Josie had only one boy interested in her—a guy who was good in math class. Fred Jacks had body odor and his hair was long and unruly. Everytime she looked at him she wondered if someday in the future he might look good. She had seen pictures of Cary Grant when he was young, and thought how unappealing he was. She wondered if Fred Jacks could turn out better than she imagined.

On Tuesday morning Josie wore a red sweater and a navy-blue skirt to school.

"You're getting so dressed up today," her mother said. Her

mother's crying had lessened and she was becoming even cheerful, but sometimes the cheerfulness felt forced. "What's the occasion?"

"Just felt like it," said Josie. Her mother smiled.

"That Freddy Jacks is just as smart as he can be," said her mother.

The first half of the day dragged, but after lunch, English class and social studies went by quickly. By three-thirty Josie was leaving the school, walking toward the park. Alice was not with her.

She saw Samuel Beckett sitting on Bench 23. He was tall, even sitting down he looked tall. He was thin and wore old pants and a clean shirt. His hair was combed, and Josie guessed his age to be about forty, though she couldn't tell for sure. She hoped she looked older than her thirteen years, and imagined she would have to admit that she had lied about her age.

"Well you certainly look older than fifteen," Mr. Beckett said upon seeing her. "If you are Josie, I would have said you were sixteen or seventeen, at least."

"Thank you." Josie sat on the bench where he had scooted over to create a space for her.

"I brought my Bible and some religious tracts." She handed him the tracts, but her hands were shaking. "You can keep those."

He slipped the papers into his shirt pocket and thanked her, but kept his eyes focused on Josie's purse, which hung from her shoulder. His eyes were bright blue and his face thin. He did not have a beard, as she had imagined, but was clean-shaven. Josie had expected him to look scruffier. He was actually handsome.

He had a low, calm voice. He sounded like a teacher now. His words were not slurred, though the whites of his eyes looked bloodshot and watery, as if he had been crying for a long time.

"So what do you want to tell me?" He was going to let her begin. He was going to listen to whatever she had to say.

"I don't know what to say," Josie began. Then she thought. "When I got saved in April, I had to walk up to the front of the tent at a Billy Graham meeting. I walked all the way."

"Did that scare you?" he asked.

"A little bit, but afterwards I felt so different. Happy, you know? I want to make everybody else feel that same way."

"I'm not sure you can do that," Mr. Beckett said. He laughed and touched her arm, the arm that held her purse, and Josie jumped. She pulled away from him.

He took a strand of her hair and pushed it behind her ear. Josie's heart leapt at his touch. What awakened in her made her body collapse inside and she grew sweaty. Her breasts felt at attention.

"Now, what do I have to do?" he asked. "There's no tent, no long walk."

"Well," said Josie. "You have to want it yourself. If you don't *want* it, it won't work." Her voice was unsteady, and her hands shaky. She felt she was doing the Lord's work, and that this was how hard it was going to be. She thought about what it would feel like if this man kissed her. She pursed her lips as she had seen women do in the movies. She felt older, sexy. She felt wild, and held tightly to her Bible.

"Maybe you don't want to be saved," she offered. "Some people just aren't interested. I have a brother named James, and he doesn't care a thing about it." Josie put the Bible on Sam Beckett's legs, and he looked down at it as though she had dropped a stone in his lap.

"Why not?" he asked her.

"James likes being bad. He thinks that if he's saved he can't be bad anymore."

"That's probably not true," said Mr. Beckett.

"I don't know," she said, "I don't think you can *want* to be bad."

"Sometimes you can't help it, though," he said. "I mean the wanting."

His words were so exciting that Josie felt trembly. His eyes grew bright looking at her, and she thought she saw his mood change. He gave her back the Bible.

"Come with me," he said, and offered his hand to lead her away. Josie followed him into a section of the park that led to a stream. She tried to walk the way she imagined Rosa would walk. She tried to pretend that she was Rosa. When they were in the trees, Sam looked around, then he put his hands on Josie's shoulders and turned her toward him.

He leaned to kiss her forehead. For the first time Josie could smell him. He did not smell like her brother, or her father. He smelled the way she imagined Africa would smell. He had the odor of fur and ground. She loved his smell.

Josie did not try to squirm away but stood very still and let Mr. Beckett run his hand down to the small of her back, over her bottom. She let him touch her breasts and thought that this might be the only man who would ever touch her. If she had her operation, and if something went wrong, then this might be her only chance for love. She let him roam around her body at will. Then he moved her toward the ground until he was almost on top of her. He looked at her for a long moment, and Josie couldn't tell what he was thinking. He looked sad. She could feel a stiffness in his groin that Alice had told her about. Alice had laughed when she told how Boog Barnett had gotten stiff at the drugstore.

Sam Beckett was kissing Josie's forehead and cheeks, but he had not yet kissed her mouth. Josie had never been kissed on the mouth, except when she was seven, and that boy had moved away. She didn't count that as a kiss, and wanted her mouth to be kissed now. She thought if she could be kissed that maybe her operation might be put off again, until after Thanksgiving, after Christmas. But when she turned her mouth toward him, Mr. Beckett stopped abruptly.

He moved to get up. "You are very young," he said.

"Por favor?" said Josie. She wondered if he had realized that she was not yet fifteen.

"You know, Josie." Beckett spoke, confused, but taking charge of himself. "You shouldn't be so willing to trust people."

"I don't trust people," she said.

"Anyway." He brushed some dirt off his arms. "I'm thinking that maybe you brought me good luck."

"Why?"

"Because I got a job after I talked with you."

"I thought you said you were a teacher," Josie questioned.

"I was. But I lost that job, and when I was out of work I just drank more than ever. I lost everything."

Josie kept wondering if he might take her money. She had

ten dollars in her purse, and she thought he might take it all. "Are you poor?" she asked.

Mr. Beckett said nothing.

"Maybe you could get back your job," said Josie. "I mean, I bet you were good." She was trying to think of a way to bring back the fervor of his previous attention, but he already seemed through with her. She didn't know what had gone wrong.

"I really was a good teacher," he said.

She could see him tear up.

"Mr. Beckett," she said, and opened her hand to him like offering a small bird. His hands were large and warm. He didn't seem old at all, and for once in her life Josie felt richer than Alice. "I have a secret," she told him.

Josie decided to tell him something she had not even told Alice, though Alice would have to know sooner or later. "You want to know what it is?"

"I guess so." Sam Beckett was smiling, but his smile seemed impatient now. He wanted to leave. "I don't have long," he said.

Josie could not believe she would tell this man what she was about to say. She licked her lips. "Four years ago the doctors found a hole in my heart, and on August tenth, they're going to operate. So when I have the operation, they don't know if I'll come through it or not, so that's partly why I decided to be saved. Because if I'm saved, then maybe God will let me live, you know? And then I can go to Africa, which is my main dream. Do you know there are animals there that people don't even know what they are?" She paused to take a breath. "And if I do *not* come through, then I figure since I'm already saved I'll go to heaven and look down on everybody, watch what people do. Maybe I can watch you, what you do. Maybe you will look through a window one day and see me there."

Her story jangled this man, visibly made him jump, and he looked at Josie Wire for a long time without speaking. He looked at her as if he were not seeing anything, but instead was seeing someone he used to know.

"How did they know about the hole in your heart?" he asked.

"I would get so tired, and blue in the face," Josie said. "My face turned blue, and my lips." She looked at Mr. Beckett. She wanted him to kiss her again. She wanted him to kiss her on the lips.

"I have a secret too," Sam said. He would give this girl the truth. "My name is not Beckett. It's Hunnicut. Bob Hunnicut. I was just teasing you when I said Beckett." He covered her hand with his.

Josie didn't think that was much of a secret, and said so. "That's more like a lie," she said.

He lifted the Bible from the ground and held it.

"I think I might like to look at this book," he told her. "I might like to read it myself."

"You would?" Josie could hardly help from asking. "Does this mean you might hope to be saved?"

"I think it *does*," he said slowly, and held out his hand. Josie shook it, pumping Bob Hunnicut's arm hard.

"I can't believe it!" she said. "Wait'll I tell Alice."

Josie began again. "Listen, my daddy's a teacher," she said. "He teaches at Webb School. Maybe you could get a job teaching there."

"Well," said Beckett-Hunnicut, "I think I better take care

of that matter myself." He stood and the length of him amazed Josie.

"You got to have *faith*," said Josie, and she stood up facing him. "*I* have faith. I am going to go to Africa someday, and see everything. Have you ever been over there?"

"No," he said.

"Listen," said Josie. "Would you kiss me? I mean, before you leave?"

Bob Hunnicut leaned over and meant to kiss Josie's forehead, but Josie at that moment turned her mouth to his mouth; and her first thought, after he kissed her, was that kissing was overrated, that it didn't feel like anything. He walked away.

As she went toward the edge of the park, Josie couldn't decide whether or not to give him all her money; but as she opened her purse he was gone. She did decide, though, to keep the secret about her defective heart awhile longer. Alice did not need to know yet. If Alice knew the truth, they could not plan to go to Africa. Josie Wire loved dreaming about Africa. She kept that dream inside her. She would love the smell of it there. She already knew what it would be like.

Stolen

The night James Hurley jumped from the bridge, his son was in bed. Sam never even heard the front door slam. Usually, whenever his father took a walk at night, Sam heard the screen door slam. He did, though, hear his father talking to his mother.

"Want to walk as far as the Market Street Bridge with me?" he asked her.

"Oh, James, not tonight," Elizabeth said. Elizabeth didn't want to leave the house so late and James knew it. The town clock had already struck ten, and she was in her nightgown.

Sam heard his father moving toward the door. He hoped they wouldn't argue again.

"Well, anyway, I'm going," he said.

"Go tomorrow night," Elizabeth told him. "I'll go with you tomorrow night."

"I'm going now. You can go, or not go."

His mood seemed casual enough, even irritated, so Elizabeth

walked with him into the yard. From the upstairs window Sam saw his father thumb back his hat, then kiss his mother, her mouth and ear. She stood while James walked to the end of the driveway, through the gate, and down the far bend of the road. From the upstairs window Sam saw him leave. He saw the white glow of his father's shirt longer than he could see his father.

During the weeks after James Hurley's funeral, state investigators asked about records missing from his office at the mill. Men came to the house to ask about the bookkeeping practices of Fred Jessup, and to question James Hurley's connection to Fred. Then, just when the asking seemed to be over, more investigators came. They walked into the yard where Sam was standing and began to question him.

"Son, did your dad bring anything into the house? Anything like a briefcase or stacks of papers?"

"Nossir. He didn't bring anything home like that." Sam grew angry as he spoke. The men were tall. They were looking toward the trash barrel. "I don't see why you're asking about my dad. He's dead. Don't you know he's dead?"

Each night, as the town's large clock belled the hours, all the mothers in Ruby, Tennessee, called their children inside for the night. But Sam liked to lie out on the hill beside his home, waiting for his father's truck to pull around the bend. As soon as he saw the truck's headlights, Sam leapt up and raced toward the gate at the end of their driveway. Even after the funeral Sam wanted to wait for his father's truck.

James Hurley knew Sam was waiting to race the truck, and

had promised not to drive more than ten miles an hour when he turned toward the gate. If he forgot, and came barreling in at regular speed, he found Sam angry, running across the long slope of the hill.

"You didn't slow down," Sam yelled.

"I think you beat me anyway," James said.

Sam climbed into the right side of the truck and James drove around to the back of the house. He pulled the emergency brake to a halt, then pushed a stack of papers across the seat and brought a can of kerosene from the truck bed.

"Help me carry this stuff, Sam," he said. "I've been cleaning out trash from the office files. When Fred Jessup moved he left that mill in a real mess."

Sam lifted a load of papers and started toward the house. "Where do you want me to put them?" he asked.

"The trash barrel," his father said. "We'll burn them."

On the evening they burned the trash, Sam had asked if he could take a job at Coop Job's junkyard.

"Dad?" Sam had been planning to ask his dad this question all day. "Can I work for Coop Job this summer?" He knew his dad would like the idea of a job, but he didn't know if he would like him to work at the junkyard with Coop Job. Coop Job had been running the town's junkyard for years. He was a testy, very private man and not many people liked him.

Sam had lifted another load of papers from the truck, throwing them into the barrel, where a load of trash still smoldered. The papers caught and flamed up.

James stood ready to add more kerosene, but it wasn't needed. He set the can away from the barrel.

"Listen," said Sam. "If I got a job collecting junk from people's houses, would you drive me around to pick it up? I could take it to Coop."

"Coop say that was okay? He gonna pay you?"

"Yeah. It was his idea." Sam had worked for Coop a few weeks last fall, though he didn't tell his parents; then Coop decided to hire him again for the summer.

"I guess I could do that." James looked sideways at his son. They both held armloads of papers. "Why do you want to work down there?" he asked. "Coop Job's mostly crazy." He touched Sam's head the way he did when he was in a good mood.

"No, he's not. Anyway, I want to earn enough money to start an account at the bank. When I get enough, I'm gonna buy me a car. When I'm sixteen, I'll have a car."

"And you think five years will give you enough?"

"It won't have to be something real smart, just an old Plymouth or Dodge, but I want it to be big. I like those big ones."

James brushed away ashes that blew up around their faces. Elizabeth came out onto the back porch and called them again. They stood a few moments watching the last batch of papers burn.

"Dad, you really think I could've beat you to the gate tonight, I mean if you hadn't sped up?"

"You're fast," said James. "You can run a lot faster than I ever did. Now, stand back and let me check this fire."

Sam thought his dad was going to stir the fire, make it smaller before they went in, but instead he poured some kerosene into the barrel. The blaze flew skyward into the trees.

"That tree's going to catch fire," Sam said.

The shadows grew huge around them, like giants walking. Sumac bushes and honeysuckle perfumed the air, and a stray cat skulked at the edge of the barn.

The moon was rising full and fiery itself. Sam stood beside his father, their arms almost touching. They stood until the flames got smaller, then dwindled. His father poked the barrel with a long stick and turned to Sam. He smiled, his first smile of the night. "Let's eat," he said.

Elizabeth was lifting the roast out of the oven when they came in. She set the platter in the middle of the table, and quickly poured tea into their ice-filled glasses.

"Sam says he wants to take a job gathering junk," James announced, with not a little pride.

"First I've heard about it," his mother said, but she saw that the answer was already decided.

Summer had just begun and school was out. Everything Sam did felt promising.

Sam had met Coop Job the previous August while looking through the junkyard for a steering wheel that might fit his go-cart. Sam and two friends had already stolen a couple of hubcaps from the yard, and some pretty fair tires. Coop owned one of those worthless junkyard dogs, but the dog had been sick and was at the vet, so for almost all of August and part of September, Sam and his two friends had helped themselves to what they needed.

A sign said *Job's Yard* and had a whole spread of dead cars. The boys scrounging around the edges of the junkyard fence could pick up odd car parts without going directly into the yard, but they could scale the fence without much difficulty, and make off with rusty pistons and bearings. Coop slept inside the small shack that stood in the middle of the yard. Job's Yard was also his home.

On Labor Day weekend, Sam's best friend, Billy D., and his next-best friend, Reese, left for the beach with their families. Sam decided to scale the fence and pick up some red paint he had seen near Coop's shack. He would have the go-cart painted red when his friends returned on Monday. Lifting stuff from Job's Yard seemed easy, and the success made Sam feel alive and dangerous.

He imagined Coop would be sleeping, and that he could get in and out in a matter of moments. He didn't expect Coop to see him climb the fence, scoot toward the shack, lift the bucket of paint and a couple of brushes, and run. But the door squeaked open and a scratchy voice yelled, "Hey! Stop, thief!"

Sam did stop. He tried to think of a way to defend himself. He had told himself that Coop had so many car parts that he wouldn't miss them, but the bucket of paint was different.

"I was just borrowing it," Sam said, turning around. "I was going to bring it back."

"Like you brought back that steering wheel and those hub-caps? You mean like that?" Coop was tall but bent over. He looked older than he was.

Sam stood before him, waiting, ready to run. He held the new paintbrush in his hand, and thought of the word "red-handed." "You gonna tell my dad?" he asked.

"Don't you think I should?"

Sam put down the bucket. "Did you really say, 'Stop, thief!'? That's what they say in old movies." Sam still held the paint-brush, but placed it now beside the bucket. He hoped he could change the subject.

"I watch a lot of those old ones," said Coop.

"That must've been where you got it."

"Guess so. Anyhow, you stopped. That must be what you are—a thief."

"I'm not either."

"Well, let's see, you stole hubcaps, a steering wheel, some leather off the cars at the back of the lot."

"You couldn't have used that leather for anything."

"That's beside the point, we're talking about what you stole. There's the paintbrush, the paint, and a rearview mirror from that old Chrysler. You're nothing but a thief."

"I am not."

"What *are* you then?"

"I'm an *American*."

"If that ain't the goddamn truth," Coop said. He thought a minute. "Guess I got several choices: I could call your daddy. I could call the police." Sam's face turned white with fear. He hadn't realized how bad this could become. "Or," said Coop, "I could *hire* you. I guess if I'm gonna *keep* anything around here, I'd better *hire* you."

Sam couldn't believe it. "You mean you would *pay* me?"

"I'll have to pay you, so's the junk won't look so good to you anymore."

"It'll look good anyway," said Sam, teasing.

"You steal from me while I'm paying you and I'll slap your ass in jail," Coop said.

"Naw, I wouldn't do that," Sam promised.

"Probly ought to anyway. You'll be robbing banks by the time you're sixteen."

"Nuh-uh. I'm all right. Listen, am I hired?"

"I guess. I guess I'm hiring your sorry American ass. Be here after school three days a week and Saturday mornings, nine o'clock. But not on Mondays. We're closed Mondays."

Sam turned to leave. "O-*kay*," he said.

"Put that paintbrush and bucket back where you found them. You want them after a week, I'll take it out of your pay."

"And you won't tell my dad?" Sam asked.

"Tell him what?" said Coop, smiling.

That was last fall.

Sam had gone to the junkyard to ride with Coop in his truck and collect junk. He liked being around him, and wanted to be the kind of person Coop Job could trust.

When Billy D. and Reese came back from the beach, they asked if they could help out at the junkyard too. They were jealous of Sam's job. But Coop said that only Sam was hired, though during the fall he let them all ride with him in the back of the truck. Billy D.'s father teased Sam about working at the yard. He said Coop was crazy.

"He's not crazy," said Sam. "He just likes to stay off alone."

After the funeral, rumors about James Hurley flew around town, and all through Hamilton County. The newspapers were full of his death, and of his association with Fred Jessup. Sam hated the whispering, but he hated even more the silence that rose whenever he entered the drugstore or barbershop. He tried to act cheerful, but nothing could make the rumors stop. Words, like invisible giants, thrummed the corners of his mind and made him feel transformed, wasted. He hardened himself against the town. He wanted to do something that would change everyone's way of looking at him.

"Did some men come by your house the other night?" Coop asked. "Did they ask about your dad?"

"They came by." Sam held his breath

"They came by here too," Coop told him.

"What'd you tell them?" Sam asked.

"I said James Hurley was a good man, and that you worked for me. That's why they came by here, they knew you worked for me. They asked me what *you* had said."

"All I told them when they came to the house"—Sam shifted on his feet—"was that Dad came home late sometimes on Wednesdays. What's wrong with that?"

"Probly shouldn't have told them anything. They're looking for any kind of clue. Anything at all."

"If you think my dad did something wrong, you better think again," said Sam. "Those men came out to the house like he was a crook or something."

"Crook? Now who sounds like an old movie? Anyhow, a man won't have to be a crook to do something wrong. You stole from me, but you're not a crook. You just needed something, or thought you did, and took it."

"But my dad wouldn't take anything. What happened was: Mr. Jessup took money from the mill, and my dad had to straighten the mess. He had to burn all the papers."

Coop stood and put on his cap. "Did you tell anybody about what your daddy burned?"

"Not yet."

"I don't think I'd tell that if I was you."

"You think he's guilty, don't you? You're just like everybody else. I thought you believed me, but you're just like everybody else. I think you're jealous because my dad had a good job and you don't have anything but this *dump* where you have to work, and where you have to sleep too. You don't even have a *house*!" Sam yelled, leaning forward, his head bobbing like a chicken. As he turned to leave, he felt an incalculable tenderness.

"Don't get all riled now," Coop spoke softly. "I'm just saying what other people might think. I never said I believed any of it. I know what a good man your daddy was." Coop went to get some papers from his desk. "This place is all I got," he said.

Sam began to look around the shed, seeing for the first time where Coop sat, where he smoked his cigarettes, where he slept and read magazines in bed, and where he drank his liquor.

He saw a sheet of tablet paper with a poem on it. "Is this your poem?"

"I'm sending it to my niece," Coop said. "Her name's Katie, and she lives in Kentucky. She likes it when I write poems for her." He took the page from Sam's hands. "I've been trying to think—what comes 'like a thief in the night'?"

"Death," said the boy. He seemed to remember this answer from church.

"Is that it? I thought it was something else. Maybe sleep."

"Nope. It's death."

"Well, death won't fit," said Coop.

"What do you mean?"

"Well, for instance if 'thief in the night' was love, I could rhyme more with love than with death."

"Make it love, then. Hell, she won't know. How old is she?"

"She's about your age," Coop said, "maybe a little older. She *thinks* she's in love."

"Maybe she is," said Sam. "Is she pretty?"

"Sure. You been in love yet?" Coop asked. "Or is it too early to think about girls?"

"Naw. I have some girls who like *me,* though."

"What makes you think they do?"

"They write me notes at school," said Sam, "and one stomped my foot."

Coop nodded in agreement.

"And one put a brownie in my lunch box."

"That's the one I believe I'd pay attention to," said Coop.

"She let me kiss her too," said Sam, but he knew Coop didn't believe anything beyond the brownie.

At night Sam's dreams turned gaudy. His father's face—without a body—kept coming up out of the river. And Sam dreamed about burning bridges, and himself burning the Market Street Bridge, seeing that bridge fall into the water, hissing.

He heard his mother tell someone that they might move away. They had never lived anywhere but Ruby, Tennessee, and Sam couldn't imagine living anywhere else. He heard his mother call her kinfolk in both California and Texas. He heard her say that she would need a job, that she wasn't afraid of working, and that Sam could get a job too.

"I *have* a job," Sam said. "I already have one at the junkyard. I bet I could ask for a raise."

"You won't be there forever," his mother said.

As the summer was ending, Billy D. and Reese asked Sam to go to the beach with them. Sam liked the idea. He thought that if he went away, maybe the rumors would be gone when he came back; but he hated thinking of his mother alone in the house, so he told Billy D. that Coop was leaving for Kentucky to visit his niece (which was true), and that he had asked Sam to watch the junkyard and feed the dog (which was partly true—the part about feeding Bud).

"How long will Coop be away?" his mother asked. They were sitting down to supper.

"About a week," Sam said.

Each night at dinnertime, Sam tried to be in the kitchen before his mother had time to call him. Sometimes she would call out his father's name, then remember and have to wait a few minutes before she could gain composure. She'd call out, "James, honey. Time to eat. Sam?" Then her face would look blank as a plate. She looked deaf for a moment.

So Sam stayed in the kitchen, and neither mentioned the empty chair, the empty house.

"Are we going to move away from here?" Sam asked. "I hate thinking we might leave."

"Maybe we won't," she said. She looked around the walls as if she could see James on the walls, in the air. They sat down, and Sam helped himself to some rolls.

"Mr. Job went to Kentucky to visit his brother and niece," Sam told his mother. "He likes his niece a lot. He writes poems for her, and sometimes I help him."

"I'd like to see that," his mother said. She smiled and Sam wondered what was funny.

•   •   •

After dinner Sam went out to the slope of the hill and watched the stars. He pretended his dad was coming home and that he was getting ready to run down the road to meet him. He lay on his back looking for the Big Dipper, the North Star, and red Mars, until his mother called him in. Sometimes he went back out, late, to watch the August meteor showers. He liked to predict the moment before a star would fall. When he was right, he felt in charge of his mind. He tried to think of what to do to make his life different, to change everything back into what it was. He wanted to stop people whispering about his father. He wanted to stop them before he went back to school.

Elizabeth called Sam inside. He brushed his teeth and told his mother good night. When she said she would come in later and kiss him, he told her not to. He was too big for that, he said.

He waited until he saw her light go off before he sneaked out of the house and down the road toward the junkyard. He wondered if Coop would be there. He wanted to tell Coop about an old motor he had seen in the mayor's backyard, and hoped Coop might say what a good man his dad was.

The shack seemed empty and Sam looked around at the bed and stove, the thin rug. He had never been inside the shack before without Coop. The room smelled like Lysol and pine cleaner, cigarettes and hard drink. Bud slept in the corner but came over to Sam.

"Hey, boy. You lonesome?" Sam rubbed the dog's ears and head. "You didn't expect me to come here tonight, did you, boy?" Sam thought how happy he would be if his father came home in the middle of the night, surprising him, saying everything was okay.

Sam sat on Coop's bed, but even here, even in this shack, he could hear the voices of the town. His mother cried all the time, and Sam didn't know how to make her stop. The voices kept curling in his mind.

Beside the door sat a can of kerosene and some rags. Coop hadn't burned his trash yesterday and Sam decided to do it for him. He soaked rags in kerosene, and threw them into a barrel piled high with unwanted items; then he poured kerosene on top and got matches that Coop kept under the steps. He lit one, but burned his hand and dropped it.

A quick flame whooshed along the ground up the side of the barrel. Trash and rags began to burn wildly. Sam kicked dirt over the ground fire, then threw handfuls of dirt onto the barrel. The flames wouldn't stop. He dug into the ground, getting dirt that was moist, and pitched big clods onto the fire. Nothing quenched the flames, and the barrel began to roar as if it might explode. The air around Sam began to grow hot. Bud hovered near the gate, barking, and Sam went to open it. He could smell kerosene on his shoes, so he slipped them off and ran barefoot toward home. The fire was all over the ground, burning toward the crowd of cars.

"C'mon, Bud." Bud loped along beside him, still barking. An explosion broke the air. As Sam turned, he saw flames covering the cars; one car exploded, then another.

Sam stopped and told Bud, "Stay, stay." He ran back to the shack, where he grabbed Coop's family pictures and the letters from his niece. He could hear the cars exploding in a domino effect, and when he left, the sky had turned light as day. Flames spread to surrounding trees, moving close to the shack. Smoke billowed high and heat began to melt portions of the fence.

Sam saw flames progressing across the field like a huge beast let loose. He couldn't believe the magnitude of what he had done. As he ran home, he could hear the whine of a siren from town. Bud kept running in circles.

"C'mon, Bud. C'mon."

As he approached his house, Sam heard three more explosions. He entered the kitchen to see his mother rushing downstairs, tying the sash of her robe. She didn't even notice that Sam was already dressed.

"You hear that?" Elizabeth said. "Sounds like a war." She moved to the window. The dog barked with every new explosion.

"What is happening?" she said softly. "Looks like it's the junkyard."

They could hear fire trucks going toward Coop's place. Bud hid under the porch, and Sam ran out to see the spectacle from the hill. His mother followed in her nightgown and robe.

She stood beside Sam. He breathed in the deep odor of sleep on her robe. Sam pointed to the smoke and fire rising now above the trees. Even trees in the woods near the junkyard burned high with flames.

"I'm glad Coop's away," said Elizabeth. She turned suddenly to look at Sam. Her whole body turned to see him, and her robe dragged the ground, gathering dirt at the hem. Sam did not want her to look at him. He did not want to see her face.

The fire had grown hot even as far as their house, and Sam wondered if their own house might burn, or if they would move away even if it didn't burn. There were so many questions not yet answered.

"Where are your shoes?" his mother asked.

He made a sound in his throat, and could only hope that his shoes had burned up, completely, along with everything else. Sam tried to picture how he might answer questions asked of him now: if he would lie, or tell the truth.

"I don't know," he said. "I took them off."

His mother's voice grew stern, and her body flexed itself tight. "I think this was an ac-ci-dent." She spoke slowly, as if Sam wasn't there.

"I think I left my shoes at the junkyard," Sam said, trying to be truthful.

"Well."

"What do you think Coop will do?" The question surprised him, even as he asked it.

"I don't know," his mother answered. She kept looking toward the fire engines and the crowd gathering at Coop's Yard. Her voice took on an edge of sadness. "But we'll have to move away now. We'll have to leave." Her words felt accusatory— accusations moving through this family like some contagious disease. A tangle of hope sped past him like a ghost.

Elizabeth put her hand on his shoulder, and Sam closed his eyes to feel circled by the warm odor beneath her robe. He covered his face with his arms, shielding himself from heat and light, and the high noise from town. A mild breeze blew the silk of her robe around his arms and legs.

Sam did not want to know what else could be stolen. He did not want to see the thieves that were everywhere.

Bargains in the Real World

Ernie wrote a letter to his wife on the computer, but the computer lost it, and as he tried to reconstruct what he had said, he found that he couldn't retrace the words. Mrs. Lamb from the next office came in to help him.

"Sometimes these things get a virus," said Mrs. Lamb. "Do you think your machine has a *virus?*" She spoke the word as though it had a foreign meaning.

"I don't think so." Ernie Bosch had just come back from having lunch with his son, Joel. He had told Joel that the divorce papers were complete, and that he planned to marry Rose in the fall. Rose was the woman he had been seeing for the past year.

"What about Mom?" Joel asked.

"She'll probably marry again too."

"You mean I'll have *two* sets of parents?" Joel spoke with a tinge of disgust, but his body sat like a fortress, private and wordless. He shared with his father an indisputable ability to concede, and though he didn't say it, he felt renounced.

Ernie saw this, and thought of all the times he had sat beside Joel and vowed to be different for him. If Ernie had to guess, he would say that his life now was due to his own ignorance about things. Ernie never blamed others for what happened, though he blamed himself doubly. His life was like a dress rehearsal; he expected it to not go well.

Mrs. Lamb pushed more buttons on the computer, trying to find the letter Ernie had written. She knew that Ernie and Janice were separated, but she never asked any questions.

Ernie had just turned fifty. He was short and slightly overweight. He had been bruised by the world but wasn't conscious of his bruises. His clothes had a ramshackle appearance, and for that reason looked too big for him. His hands lay flat and large like sycamore leaves, and since his divorce, his pant legs crept up above his ankles. People worried about him. He walked around in an uncollected state of mind.

"Look," Mrs. Lamb remarked, "Joel's here." Ernie looked up to see Joel in the doorway. And though Joel hadn't said anything, his face looked as if a brushfire had swept over it—bare and raw as burned ground.

"Lucas Wiley's gone," Joel said. Lucas was Joel's best friend. He always threatened to run away, and his parents spoke of these threats without believing them.

"What do you mean?" Ernie asked.

"He left. That's it. That's just what I mean." Joel sounded angry with his father, and Mrs. Lamb slipped quietly into her own office. Joel still had on his coat, and Ernie lifted his own from the coatrack. They walked to the car.

"I knew it when we were having lunch," said Joel. "I probably would have told you, but what you said about divorce made me forget. Then I got back to school and everybody was scared. Lucas left a note." He looked at his father. "Like a suicide or something. There was police and everybody asking questions. I didn't say what I knew, or even that I knew anything."

"Did anybody ask you?"

"No. Not police. Some people, though, said did I know. I said I didn't know where he went, and that part was true."

They arrived at the car and Joel waited for his father to unlock his side.

They got in. "You should say if you know anything."

"I know where he *might* be. I know he might be one of two places."

"Where's that?"

"He likes to go to a place way back in the woods, and he keeps beer there, sometimes whiskey, and he gets drunk sometimes, but it doesn't take much for him to get drunk. I think he just *acts* like it."

Ernie wondered if Joel did this too, but it wasn't the time to ask. He started the car and asked where this place was, and where Joel thought the other place was. Ernie said they would look in both places. He said Joel had to tell what he knew, because Lucas was the kind of boy who might hurt himself, and maybe they could protect him from it.

Ernie Bosch was not a man of action, but he was a man of

principle. He found the will to act if there was a reason, and if the reason resulted in protecting someone. He left his marriage because he no longer loved his wife. He wanted to protect her from spending a bad life with him.

He made the decision to marry Rose because she needed him. She said she didn't know what would happen if he wasn't around. Ernie protected Joel in all the ways he knew, and now he would try to keep Lucas from performing something regretful. They drove five miles outside town to the edge of Barrow's Pond, and walked from there into the woods.

"He walk all this way?"

"He walks all this way all the time. His parents don't care."

The woods had the smell of rain. The ground around the pond was soggy, even with the dry spell that had come in September. Ernie tried to think of what they might encounter if they found Lucas. He tried to think how they would find him.

In the restaurant where they had eaten lunch two hours ago, Ernie had waited for Joel to walk from school. He sat in the queasy smell of long-cooked food and talked with the waitress whose name was Viola—though her name was spelled wrong on the tag she wore over her big left breast, and instead read *Voila*.

When Joel finally came into the restaurant and sat down, they ordered tuna cheese melts. Viola brought them Cokes.

"I have something to say," Ernie said, deciding to blurt it out. He couldn't think of what else to do. "I'm going to get married again."

Joel knew Rose, and he knew his father had been seeing her, but he didn't like her. He didn't like the way she smelled, like biscuit dough. "Why?" he asked.

"Well, we like each other a lot." Ernie scooted around in his chair. "I don't want anything to be different between *us*, though." His words sounded hollow, stupid.

"Is she gonna move in to your apartment?" Joel spent weekends with his dad, and wondered now what would happen to their weekends.

"No. But her house is big, and far enough out that we can hunt dove and even deer on the land out there."

Ernie fell in love with Rose at the beginning of the summer, though he had known her for seven years and knew her husband before he died. Rose took care of him in ways that Janice could never do, and she had a sweetness that almost never crossed him. He thought he could be around someone like that forever. It might even be easy.

"Did you tell your mother you were coming out here with me?" Ernie walked behind Joel, letting him lead the way into the woods.

"Yeah, I told her we might go looking for Lucas." He spoke as if Ernie had no right to ask anything about his mother.

There was a path that Joel was following, though at times the path turned into no path at all, then picked up again.

Ernie followed, but looked up to see a scattering of clouds, and sky moving away in every direction. He tried to get a picture in his head of how it might be when the distance burned away and he was left standing alone. He wondered sometimes if this had already happened.

"I haven't been here since last summer," Joel said.

They were headed toward a specific place, and though Ernie

had been in these woods before, he did not recognize landmarks today. He watched Joel's long strides, his small, wiry body carrying the burden of being thirteen.

They shifted through the brush and sticky branches, avoiding broken places in the ground until Ernie saw, and Joel pointed to, a shack leaning and almost fallen. Ernie opened the makeshift door carefully, because the whole structure looked as though it might collapse in moments. He didn't want to go inside, and told Joel not to.

"It's all right," Joel said. He was in a good mood now. "It's sturdier than it looks." He pushed the wall to show its sturdiness. The wall did not budge.

"He's not here." Joel spoke with disappointment, but then he saw a few schoolbooks and Lucas's book bag in the corner and said, "Maybe he is."

"You think he heard us coming?" Ernie asked.

Joel gazed around for other evidence of Lucas. "He won't like to have somebody else in here. Even me. He told me once I couldn't come back, because I brought another person with me. He said I broke the code. Anyhow, he won't let me back in. I haven't been here since summer."

Joel sat on the floor of the shed. In the corner lay a small pallet where Lucas sometimes slept. Sheets were tucked neatly around the pallet, and a crate beside it had a clock and a portable radio.

"Looks real homey," Ernie said to no one.

Ernie had to admit that in this shed there existed a dark, protective peace. He wanted to sit down and stay awhile. He wanted to see what was so simply felt. The floor was made of old wood boards, pink with dust and spangled with light that fell through the cracks. The rays of dust extenuated his feeling of shadowy peace. It was not a calmness. Instead, all his senses felt heightened, as fear does sometimes, or sickness. He felt alive, adrift, afire.

"What's the matter?" Joel asked. "You look funny."

"I'm just thinking," Ernie lied. "I'm just trying to figure out where Lucas might be. Maybe we should wait for him here."

"He's gonna be mad," Joel warned.

"I think we should wait." Ernie spoke with the authority of a father who knows just what to do in such situations.

The floor was swept clean with the dust of years settled on the boards, and Ernie let his hands rest in the softness of the wood. He had never felt like this before. He was afraid he might never feel this way again.

Lucas Wiley's parents were not real parents. They owned a big house in a section of town reserved for the very rich. Joel visited Lucas there and met Mrs. Wiley, a lawyer—thin, her face dimmed by a miserable spirit. He met Mr. Wiley, who served on the city council and sold real estate. Lucas's real parents died in a car wreck four years earlier. The Wileys adopted him out of pity, and out of their own wish for a child. They expected Lucas to be grateful. They did not expect him to cause the kind of trouble that he caused regularly.

Ernie knew about Lucas. He had studied his case, even before Joel grew to be his friend. Ernie worked at the Board of

Education as special assistant to the superintendent. His promotion a few years ago was due to a speech he wrote, called "The Ten Tenets of Education." And though the speech was without much imagination, it was simple and direct enough to hit the hearts of school officials. Ernie traveled around the state to deliver his speech, and once the speech was photocopied and sent out to superintendents in other states. Now Ernie couldn't remember even one of the tenets that had made him so famous.

Joel hadn't said anything for several minutes, then he spoke. "Dad, are you really gonna get married?"

"What?"

"Mom came to school and brought me my gym shorts, and when I told her about you she didn't know anything about it." He spoke as though this statement might nullify Ernie's plan to marry Rose.

"No, she didn't know. I wanted to tell her myself. I forgot to tell you I wanted to say it myself."

"Well, she knows now. But she thinks maybe you're just *thinking* about getting married, and that probably you won't do it at all."

Ernie wondered if Janice could be right. She was often right about such things. He would have to speak to her about Rose, and the prospect of this meeting made him depressed. He dreaded hearing her reproaches. He wanted to tell Janice that he was sorry, and to say that Rose was the one he loved.

The door swung open and a huge yellow dog came barreling in, stumbling and barking at these strangers. The dog's head was larger than any Ernie had ever seen on a dog. Not exactly his head, but his face. His face was larger than normal.

Lucas came in behind the dog. He carried a gun and a rabbit he had shot, and a bag of food from McDonald's.

"Hey, Lucas!" Joel spoke quickly and with such friendliness that Lucas was caught off guard and didn't see, at first, Ernie standing behind Joel. "We thought you were gone."

Lucas saw Ernie. "What are you here for, Mr. Bosch?" He was polite. Lucas knew how to be polite. He pretended that nothing was wrong.

"Everybody's worried about you," Ernie said. "They found your note."

"So what?"

"So, they don't know where you are."

"So I'm here." He was surly, not polite at all. "What're you going to do?"

"We're not going to do anything," Joel said. "We're just seeing where you are."

Theirs was one of those friendships, anyone could see, where one boy thinks the world of the other, and the other hardly notices the one who worships him. The dog had been shooed out but came back now, and the shed was suddenly and irrevocably crowded. The dead rabbit lay in the corner next to the book bag, and the dog went for it, growling as though the rabbit might still be alive. Lucas and Joel yelled, and pounded the dead animal away from the dog's mouth.

"Get outa here, Galilee," Lucas yelled. Galilee went just outside the door to lie down. "He nearly tore it to pieces." Lucas held up the bloody rabbit. "I might as well give it to him now." He threw the rabbit out the door, and Galilee carried it into the woods to feast.

"You want some of this food?" They sat down in a circle and Lucas opened the white McDonald's bag. Ernie wanted to mention that he should wash his hands first, but nothing seemed appropriate in a usual way, so they each took whatever sandwich Lucas gave. They ate, sharing one large drink. Ernie refused anything to drink until he had finished his sandwich, then took a few sips. He praised the shed, and Lucas could tell that everything Mr. Bosch said, he meant.

While they were sitting there, something incredible happened. The sun was going down, so there was no reason for there to be so much light. But for what seemed a full minute, a light came in from an angle higher than where the sun was. Spangles of light flew all around them, moving and jerking like some old-time ballroom dance floor. And the effect was one of intense movement or a jerky movie, so that nothing seemed real, except for the moment.

The experience was like a dream Ernie sometimes had: when the mind would light on an image for a longer than usual time. And in the dream a shimmer surrounded the moment, so that when Ernie woke he could remember the shimmer but couldn't describe it very well. Now, in the shed, the same kind of dopey motion came in. And while the light was so furious around them, they stayed quiet, attentive, as if they could hear a voice speak. Galilee entered and stood very still, not barking. His yellow presence sealed the experience for them. They felt balanced by his full head.

When it was over Lucas said, "Did you hear anything?" and Ernie said he didn't, but he wouldn't have been surprised if he had. Joel didn't answer, then Lucas said he had heard something and it was like a voice, but not outside his head. He said he heard it speak.

"What'd it say?" Joel asked him.

"It said to bury something." Lucas looked slightly weary when he said this. Weary and puzzled. "It said, 'Bury the bones. Find the bones and bury them.' " And he got up as if he might be ready to do such a thing.

"What bones?" Joel asked him, not completely surprised.

"I don't know."

Ernie thought how strange this was, and he thought, too, that maybe Lucas had been drinking, but he didn't smell any liquor. "So what do you think, then?" Ernie asked.

"We have to find bones somewhere," Lucas said. He included all of them in his plan.

Joel stood up. "We do?"

"Yeah, because when I heard it, I saw the place in my mind. It's near the edge of the pond on the other side."

Ernie decided to play along, though he also felt he believed Lucas completely. As they walked toward the pond, Joel said, "I heard it too."

Ernie did not believe Joel but said nothing.

"I *did*," said Joel. "I heard it and know exactly where we're going."

And at that moment Ernie realized that he, too, had a picture of where they were headed, though he had not been on this side of the pond before. This side of the pond belonged to the Johnsons' nephews, and they had posted "No Trespassing" signs everywhere. The Johnsons did not approve of hunting, so hunters avoided the Johnson side of the pond. Still, Ernie knew what the place looked like, but he didn't admit his knowledge. He wanted to see if the picture in his head would match up to the real thing.

Galilee tagged along, but as they moved onto the Johnsons' land, he loped ahead and came upon a small clearing that was exactly what Ernie had pictured, and Joel said, "That's it."

Lucas nodded. The clearing had tall, thin trees surrounding it, and in the middle they could see where a large tree had been cut down, leaving a space about the size of a small room. Grass had begun to sprout on the forest floor.

There were bones on the ground, and Ernie, when he saw them, felt amazed. "What do you know about this?" Ernie spoke as though he planned to interrogate both boys.

"Nothing," Lucas said. "I came here because of what just happened in the shed." There was nothing frantic or untrue in his voice, so Ernie turned to Joel.

"And you?"

"I never even been here before. Not to this place. I been all over everywhere else, though." The bones lay at their feet and Ernie lifted one. It felt dry and brittle in his hands.

Galilee walked around the bones, then wandered off to find a small piece of cloth stuck to a man's glove, and brought it to them. The glove was intact, but the cloth was covered with muddy leaves and small white bugs.

Lucas grew excited. He stuck his hand inside the glove, so that one hand looked like a clown's. "Let's bury the glove too," he said. "No telling whose this was." He put it on the ground beside the bones.

"These bones look like a deer or a cow, or something," said

Ernie, "but I guess we should report it, don't you? I mean, since we're burying them, we should say something. I'm just wondering how we'll say we found it. How will we tell it?"

"Say Galilee found it!" Joel suggested. "Say he came and got us and made us come here. Say he barked and went crazy till we did." Joel's voice grew excited with possibilities. Lucas didn't deny that they should say this. He didn't mind using Galilee for an excuse. They needed a reason other than the spangles of light.

Lucas folded the cloth into a soft wad. His eyes had the meekness of someone in love.

"Let's get to work." Ernie spoke with authority, but Lucas and Joel had already begun to dig a hole with their hands.

Lucas had been adopted several months after his family was killed by a truck crashing into their car. They were returning home from a visit to his uncle in Comer, Georgia, when Lucas was ten years old. The truck driver believed that everyone in the car was dead when he went to get help, but Lucas had crawled out the back window, alive. He had seen his family scattered and unrecognizable.

Lucas did not go to the funeral, or to the graveside service. He had refused to see his family in so many coffins, wanting instead to keep them in his mind as they were before they were buried, but his unfortunate decision had made it impossible to let them go.

Once, when Lucas was suspended from school for running away, Mrs. Wiley brought him to the superintendent's office, but they went to Ernie's office first. When Lucas tried to defend himself to Mr. Bosch, Mrs. Wiley said, "You don't live in the real world, Lucas."

Lucas thought he knew the real world better than anyone. He had seen it. He had stood for a long while looking at his family before anyone came. "You're not my real mother," Lucas said back to her.

Ernie and Joel dug a hole with sharp rocks and scooped dirt with their hands. They placed the bones into the hole, then the glove, and Lucas made a cross with two sticks. He wrapped the sticks with a vine to make the shape of the cross sturdy. Ernie helped build a mound so the place would resemble a grave, and Joel put leaves and sections of moss on top. It seemed to Ernie that the boys had done this kind of thing before. They worked together in a way that looked practiced.

"It's probably an animal of some kind," Ernie said, but now Lucas and Joel enjoyed the pretense that it might be a person.

"There," said Lucas. "I guess we should pray or something."

"I guess so." Joel put the last of the dirt onto the bones. He placed the piece of cloth at the foot of the grave. "Who's gonna do it?"

Ernie didn't offer. He had not prayed for anything in a long time.

"*I* will," said Lucas, surprising everyone. They bowed their heads, and Lucas shifted his feet into a sure place on the ground.

"Oh Lord," he began, knowing how to begin, "there has been somebody here that you know, and that we have buried. We think it is some man, or woman. So now, if you take them up with you, and if you wish their souls to come from the ground, then we will be glad to have participated in this thing. And we don't know how to explain what has happened. So if you can tell us how to say it, and what to do, then people will know we've done what's right. Because we will not ever forget this place and how it all came to pass here. And now we hope nothing bad happens again, not to anyone we know, or don't know. And when we go home please make us heroes in the town so that people will say our names," and he added, "on the radio."

They held their silence, and could smell the cool odor of earth. When they looked up, Galilee stood with his head still bowed. He was chewing on the cross.

When they got back to town, the time was past six o'clock. They went straight to Sheriff Munsy's office—a hot, airless room off Seventh Street. They told how they had come across bones in the woods, and buried them. Their voices sounded haggard and proud as they told it, and the sheriff listened, along with two other men in the office.

"Did you see anybody else out there?"

"No, sir."

"Well, I mean, what made you go out to the Johnson land? It was posted, right?"

"We were looking for Lucas," Ernie explained, but he didn't mention the shed or the spangled light. "Joel and I went looking for him in the woods. We saw Galilee first, then we saw Lucas. He'd been hunting rabbits out there."

"You think he had anything to do with this?" Sheriff Munsy asked the question to Ernie, but looked toward Lucas.

"No, sir. We ran across the bones coming back. Just saw them spread out on the ground." Ernie's lie came as a shock to himself, as well as to Joel and Lucas.

The sheriff spoke thoughtfully. "What kind of bones?"

"Animal," said Ernie. "Some kind of animal."

Then Joel said how he and Lucas hunted out there all the time. He said they had seen old cow bones before.

Sheriff Munsy noticed a piece of fabric hanging from Lucas's back pocket.

"What's that?" he asked and reached to lift it out. As he took the piece of cloth, Lucas's thin face grew so pained that even the sheriff knew this was nothing but a private treasure. A look of tender desperation, the face of a child who has had a favorite toy taken away. The sheriff shook the fabric over the trash can and handed it back, watching Lucas's body relax into a regular position.

"You boys stay away from the Johnson land," the sheriff warned.

Ernie and the two boys stood together like tired soldiers, as if they were making a silent bargain with the world.

"What made you run off like that, boy?" the sheriff asked.

Lucas didn't answer. He smiled, not a real one—a smile more learned than felt.

"You nearly scared us to death." Sheriff Munsy touched Lucas's shoulder. "Come on. I'll drive you home."

"No thanks, Sheriff," Ernie said. "We got Galilee outside. Anyway, I have to take Joel to his mama's. Lucas can ride with me."

"I'm gonna stay with *you* at your house tonight," Joel said. He didn't usually spend weeknights at his dad's, so the suggestion felt like a promise.

They told the sheriff good night.

Mrs. Wiley held her cat to her chest as she opened the door to see Lucas, Ernie, and Joel. Her arms looked long in her wide-sleeved robe. "Where have you been?" She spoke like a ventriloquist and stepped toward Lucas. Mr. Wiley stood back from everyone, as though he couldn't be touched.

Ernie told them everything, but nothing about the shed of light. There was only one world to live in, though there were many to experience. He spoke from the world they lived in, and never tried to explain the other.

He made what they had done sound heroic, but on the way home in the car Joel asked his father, "If we'd told them what happened in the shed, would they've believed it?"

"I don't think so."

"Lucas's parents sure looked surprised to see him," Joel said. "His mother looked *sick*."

Ernie looked off over the dark fields. He felt like a man leaving mountains that had always been familiar to him—not turning to see them again but not able to forget their shape at his back.

They pulled up to Ernie's old house, where Janice and Joel lived now. Joel went in to get his pajamas and schoolbooks. When Janice came to the door, Ernie told her that Joel would be staying with him for the night. He told her, too, that he would marry Rose in the spring.

Later, when he tucked Joel into bed, Ernie said, "If you need anything, call out. I'll leave the door open so I can hear."

"Okay, Dad." Then he said, "Listen—"

"What."

"It's all right if you marry that Rose person. I mean, it'd be good, you know? I could come out there and hunt. We'd have fun."

"Sure." Ernie patted Joel's arm. He could feel the warmth of skin through his pajamas.

"Do you think we'll get our names in the paper?" Joel asked.

"Maybe."

"Will it be on the radio, like Lucas said?"

"It might." Ernie leaned to turn off the light. "Joel, why did Lucas keep that dirty piece of cloth? Why'd he have it with him? I didn't see him pick it up, did you?"

"Whenever he finds something," said Joel, turning on his side, "he likes to pretend it belongs to his family. Like it's his mama's or something. One time he found a comb, and kept that too."

"Oh." Ernie raised his head in understanding.

"He's buried bones before," Joel confessed. "I think he does it all the time, maybe." Joel sat up in bed. "And you know that rabbit he shot? I bet he buries those bones tomorrow. I mean, if Mrs. Wiley ever lets him out of the house again." He lay back down. "I think he shoots things just to bury them. He just keeps burying and burying." Joel waited a few moments before he said, "And sometimes he lets me bury them with him." It sounded like a secret. "But mostly he does it alone." Joel's eyes went into a remembering mode. "He has little graves all over those woods. Like he's putting his family down everywhere, over and over."

Ernie pushed his fingers through Joel's hair.

"How long you think he'll keep doing that?" Joel asked the question as if he hoped it wouldn't go on much longer.

Ernie stood, nodding. "I don't know," he said, "but it seems, to me, a pretty good thing to do." He started to close the door. "Joel, do you know what Lucas wrote in that note? The one at school? Did you see it?"

Joel's voice came from the bed. "He wrote his name, I mean, his real name. He wrote: 'My name is *not Wiley*.'" When Joel said this, he underlined the air with his finger. "It said: 'My name is Lucas Sanford, and I'm hungry for luck.'"

Thinking of Lucas—his face in the woods, picturing him digging for luck—was like the difference between seeing a reflection in a window and then seeing through it. So for the rest of that night Ernie tried to understand the mad proportion of their experience. He thought of all the arbitrary forces acting together in the world, and the algebra of other worlds. Of bones underground spread out like a fortune-teller's prediction, of Lucas in a strange house, Joel in bed, and the unsleeping that went on in the dark woods.

Then Ernie closed his eyes, but before he slept he turned his head sideways, trying to bring back that shed of light, and he bargained silently for an answer. And for many nights beyond this one, Ernie wondered if it was lunacy to try and rid anybody of their old life.

ELIZABETH COX was born and raised in
Chattanooga, Tennessee. She is an associate
professor at Duke University, and has taught
creative writing at Bennington College, Boston
University, the University of Michigan, Tufts
University, and the University of North Carolina
at Chapel Hill. She is the author of three novels,
*Familiar Ground, The Ragged Way People Fall Out of
Love,* and *Night Talk,* as well as poetry, essays, and
short stories, one of which was selected for the
1994 O. Henry Award collection. Cox has
two children, Michael and Elizabeth, and lives
in Littleton, Massachusetts, with her husband,
Michael Curtis, who is senior editor of
The Atlantic Monthly.

A B O U T   T H E   T Y P E

The text of this book was set in Janson, a misnamed
typeface designed in about 1690 by Nicholas Kis,
a Hungarian in Amsterdam. In 1919 the matrices
became the property of the Stempel Foundry in
Frankfurt. It is an old-style book face of excellent
clarity and sharpness. Janson serifs are concave
and splayed; the contrast between thick and thin
strokes is marked.